'What do you think of Mr Prosser's new houseman?' Sarah whispered aside to Trina.

Trina made a face. 'Not a lot. A bit of an ogre, isn't he?'

Sarah looked surprised. 'Oh? We think he's rather dishy. He's good, too. Did an emergency appendix from Kids' ward last night that was very nasty, and made a super job of it too. His wife's lovely, a gorgeous redhead —have you seen her?'

The anaesthetist turned to ask Sarah to hold up the patient's chin and Sarah winked. This was Trina's signal to withdraw from the anaesthetic room, and she did so, with a last reassuring smile at the patient.

We think he's rather dishy. The words echoed in her ears as she changed back into her shoes outside the main theatre doors. Not my cup of tea, thanks, she thought grimly. Dr Bayne dishy? He could go and take a running jump, for all she cared. So then why did the memory of him standing at the theatre sink in his vest and operating trousers disturb her so?

Georgina Blake spent much of her childhood abroad, but returned to England in her teens to train as an SRN in the West Country where she was born. She now lives in Norfolk with her artist husband and their three children, drawing on her vivid memories of hospital life and routine for her stories. THAT HAUNTING MALADY is her first Doctor Nurse romance.

THAT HAUNTING MALADY

BY

GEORGINA BLAKE

MILLS & BOON LIMITED
ETON HOUSE 18–24 PARADISE ROAD
RICHMOND SURREY TW9 1SR

All the characters in this book have no existence outside the imagination of the Author, and have no relation whatsoever to anyone bearing the same name or names. They are not even distantly inspired by any individual known or unknown to the Author, and all the incidents are pure invention.

All rights reserved. The text of this publication or any part thereof may not be reproduced or transmitted in any form or by any means, electronic or mechanical, including photocopying, recording, storage in an information retrieval system, or otherwise, without the written permission of the publisher.

This book is sold subject to the condition that it shall not, by way of trade or otherwise, be lent, resold, hired out or otherwise circulated without the prior consent of the publisher in any form of binding or cover other than that in which it is published and without a similar condition including this condition being imposed on the subsequent purchaser.

First published in Great Britain 1988
by Mills & Boon Limited

© Georgina Blake 1988

Australian copyright 1988
Philippine copyright 1988

ISBN 0 263 75970 7

Set in 10 on 12 pt Linotron Times
03–0188–50,850

Photoset by Rowland Phototypesetting Limited
Bury St Edmunds, Suffolk
Made and printed in Great Britain by
William Collins Sons & Co Limited, Glasgow

For my mother Grace, who never gave up!

CHAPTER ONE

IF TRINA MORGAN had known what fate had in store for her when she went on duty that February morning, she might have taken a horse and a suit of armour with her and been better prepared to do battle.

And if Giles Bayne, ex-engineer—(seven years ago he'd found designing sugar-beet factories unsatisfying and discovered a burning ambition to study medicine at the relatively late age of twenty-three)—if Giles had known what kind of Joan of Arc he was about to meet in his new post as houseman at Norchester's General Hospital, he might well have taken a spiked club.

But neither of them knew—and perhaps it was just as well, because if they had known in advance what was to happen to them at precisely ten-thirteen that particular morning, the baby would never have been stolen from Maternity a week later and everything would have been different.

As it was, Trina, sublimely unaware of what was about to turn her life upside down, propped the note against the toaster on the kitchen table in her flat and stood back to survey it.

OUT OF EGGS, the note said. WILL BRING SOME IN. SLEEP WELL! LOVE, T. Would Mandy see it when she came off duty? They had promised Keith and Alan one of Mandy's fabulous omelettes each for supper that evening and, without eggs, it wasn't going to be much of a roaring triumph for anyone.

Satisfied, Trina smiled to herself. Knowing Mandy, the toaster would be the first place she headed for when she got back to the flat after a gruelling night on the Children's Ward. And if Mandy didn't see it, Sarah their other flatmate would, and tell her.

Reassured, Trina fastened her coat over her blue-checked uniform, picked up her shoulder-bag, and let herself out of the flat.

Giles Bayne had already been up since five. Considering that it had gone three when he had eventually got to bed after removing an appendix the previous evening, his temper was not at its best. He was eager to impress his consultant surgeon, a cultured gentleman of aristocratic Italian extraction several generations back—Mr Prosser had an eye for a pretty nurse owing to this Latin blood—and Giles was very much on edge that morning.

He was grabbing a quick slice of toast in his own flat as Trina left hers, both of them quite unaware that Fate was drawing them inexorably together.

The early February wind was biting, and Trina shivered, grateful for the fact that she would soon be in the comforting warmth of the hospital only a few blocks away. One thing about nursing, she thought as she turned a corner and met the icy blast head-on, you can always be sure of being warm enough on duty!

The locker room was deserted as she hung up her coat and took a fresh paper cap out of her locker. Crossing over to the mirror above the handbasins, she folded it deftly into the required shape and secured the ends together. She ran a comb through her soft dark hair and fished in her purse for the white hairclips with which to hold the cap in place. She was just in the act of positioning it neatly in the middle of her head when the door opened and Liz Burroughs came in, yawning sleepily.

'Hello, Trina. You haven't got a new cap you can let me have for tonight, I suppose? This one's absolutely had it.' Liz pulled off the one she was wearing and threw it into the nearby bin. 'I'm too exhausted to go all the way down to the office to get a new one.'

'You're lucky,' said Trina, handing over an unfolded one. 'I had the foresight to take several when Matthews handed them out on Thursday.'

'Angel!' Liz said. 'God, I'm shattered. We haven't sat down all night. I suppose you're just going on?'

Trina nodded. She finished pinning her cap into place, applied a light touch of mascara, and straightened her uniform dress. A quick glance into the mirror reflected her oval face and short straight nose above generous lips and wide-set hazel eyes that so candidly revealed her feelings. 'Any idea how busy we are?'

'On Merton?' Liz unlocked her locker door. 'I think your lot had a pretty quiet night—just as well, Prue Gant was in charge. That girl baffles me—she's an absolutely hopeless nurse, yet she's so neurotically tidy. Even if a bomb hit the ward and killed half the patients, it would still look like a museum by morning!'

Trina chuckled. Prue Gant was known for her obsessive habits. 'Well, I'm off to save lives,' she said lightly, checking that her scissors and pens were in appropriate pockets. She picked up her handbag. 'Have a good sleep. If you see Mandy Pearce when she comes off duty, tell her I've left her a note on the toaster, will you?'

'Sure.' Liz turned the key in her locker door. 'Have a good day, and don't work too hard.'

Giles swallowed the last of his toast and finished his coffee. Wishing like hell he had stayed in sugar-beet factory designing—but only briefly—he glanced at the bed. What he would give to fall into it now! Damn that stupid girl on Merton Ward—without her inane phone call he could have had a couple more hours' sleep.

But duty called, and Giles was thoroughly ambitious. Mr Prosser had a Theatre list that morning, and Giles was looking forward to getting a retractor into the scheduled cholecystectomy from Thompson Ward, not to mention the odd probable emergency. He bent to the mirror, smoothed his dark hair, and straightened his tie. The morning's case-load might be unpredictable, but Giles was ready for it.

Trina left the locker room and made her way up through the maze of corridors towards Merton Ward, the surgical ward where she worked. She glanced at the fob watch pinned to the front of her uniform. Only ten to eight. She was nice and early.

She passed the Children's Ward en route and peeped in as she passed the ward doors. Through the round windows she could see the beds and cots with their small occupants. Mandy, one of her two flatmates, was feeding a boy of about five who lay restlessly in an orthopaedic bed, his legs strung up in Gallows traction.

Trina opened one of the doors softly and peeped round into the ward. Mandy looked up and waved. The child turned lively eyes towards the opening ward door.

'Hi, Trina,' said Mandy, seeing her friend, then

turned back to the child. 'Look, Darren, if you don't hurry up and eat this Weetabix, I'll feed it to Staff Nurse instead. She knows what's good for her if you don't!'

'Go on, then!' the child said wickedly. 'I dare you!'

Mandy raised her eyes to the ceiling. 'Honestly, Trina, what do you do? This wretched creature's had me running about all night, he's so full of beans. If he wasn't tied into the bed he'd be up on the ceiling by now. But I can't get him to finish his breakfast.' She sighed. 'I don't know—kids!'

Trina winked at the child. 'If you hurry up and finish that Weetabix,' she said coaxingly, 'I'll bring you the Monster card in the bottom of the packet we've got in our flat when I come on duty tomorrow.'

'Cor!' said the child, his eyes gleaming. 'Would yer?'

'Course I will,' said Trina. 'But you'll have to eat up that bowlful for Staff Nurse Pearce first.'

'Right on!' Darren said eagerly. He grabbed the spoon out of Mandy's hand and ate the rest of the cereal at once.

'Bribery and corruption,' grinned Mandy gratefully. 'But who cares, so long as it does the trick? You little horror,' she added to the child, 'I bet you'd have eaten it anyway, wouldn't you?'

'Course I would,' Darren said cheerfully. 'I like Weetabix, don't I? My mum always gives it to me at home.'

'Grrrr!' said Mandy, grinning at him. She got up reluctantly from her chair. 'Oh, am I looking forward to bed!'

'I'd better go,' said Trina, looking at her watch. 'It's three minutes to. I'll see you later. I've left a note to say I'll bring in some eggs for your famous omelettes when I come home—we're completely out of them. Go and sleep the sleep of the just. You look as if you need it.'

'Thank goodness I'm nights off tonight,' Mandy yawned. 'See you!'

Waving, Trina left the Children's Ward and quickened her pace along the corridor. As she arrived at the doors of Merton Ward, her watch said just before eight.

She went through the main ward doors, waved to a couple of the men who weren't screened off by their bed-curtains in one of the male patients' cubicles, and approached the nurses' station. Merton was a mixed-patient ward, with both male and female cubicles, six beds in each. The nurses' station was positioned centrally, with a good view down the corridor both ways and into the glass-walled cubicles.

Prue Gant was sitting neatly at the central desk, looking as trim as if she had just come on duty instead of being in charge of a hectic ward for the last twelve hours. Her hands roamed restlessly across the desk top, righting papers and setting the Kardex into a precise position in the centre.

'Morning, Prue,' Trina said cheerfully, hanging her handbag on one of the pegs nearby. 'Had a good night?'

There was no answering greeting, and Trina turned back to the desk with surprise, realising suddenly that Prue Gant's upright back and meticulously groomed appearance were shaking.

'Whatever's the matter?' asked Trina with concern. She looked at Prue's face. It was blotchy with tears. 'Are you all right?'

Prue Gant's eyes filled with fresh tears. 'Oh, Staff, I've had a terrible night! I've had a dreadful time with Mr

Prosser's houseman . . .' Her face crumpled and she began to cry afresh.

'With Dr Rodney?' Trina echoed, amazed. 'But why, for heaven's sake? She's always marvellous.'

'No, not Dr Rodney,' Prue said tearfully. 'There's a new one—a horrible man. I had to call him out to see Mr Wallace at half past two, and he was absolutely p-poisonous . . .'

'Whatever happened?' Trina asked, alarmed. It was unheard-of that a doctor should be angry at being asked to see a patient if he was on call. She thought of Mr Wallace, who was a six-day post-operative prostatectomy—in fact, one of the men who had waved to her as she had come through the door and along the corridor, so he must be all right.

'He couldn't sleep,' Prue said tearfully. 'I'd given him his night sedation at ten, but it hadn't worked by two-thirty, so I rang the houseman on call . . .'

Oh dear, thought Trina, her heart sinking. Aloud she said, 'Go on.'

'I rang him and asked if he could come and change Mr Wallace's sedation.' Prue sniffed miserably. 'Yes, all right, I know I should have left it until morning really, but if you've ever lain awake all night, you'd know how terrible it is. So I rang him.'

'What did he say?'

'He swore at me down the telephone,' Prue sniffed. 'He told me I was an inefficient nincompoop and to give the man a cup of tea and that he'd change the prescription in the morning.'

'So that was all right, then,' Trina said with relief.

'No, it wasn't. After I'd put the phone down he came to the ward after all. But by that time I'd given Mr

Wallace a cup of tea and he was sound asleep. So sound asleep he was snoring!'

Oh dear, thought Trina. 'And this Dr Whatsit—he was annoyed, was he?'

'Annoyed?' Prue bit her lip. 'He was absolutely blazing! He went and peered at Mr Wallace, and then he came into Sister's office where I was sitting, and said all kinds of horrible things to me like I had no consideration at all for the medical staff, and that I was a useless ninny. He changed Mr Wallace's night sedation in a foul mood, then he stormed off again saying that if I called him again for anything less than a burst abdomen he'd personally tip a bottle of Tuinal down the back of my dress!'

Trina stifled a smile. 'But he needn't have come down,' she pointed out. 'It was his decision to do so, after all. You weren't to blame.'

'But he was so horrible,' sniffed Prue. 'I do worry a lot about the patients, I know—probably more than I should, but it's difficult to think of the right thing to do when someone can't sleep and you know they must be feeling awful.'

Trina put her arm round Prue's thin shoulders. 'I know you worry about them,' she said kindly. 'Nobody could be more conscientious than you are, so you're not to get upset about it. If he comes in this morning, I'll have a word with him and explain what went wrong, don't worry.'

'Would you, Staff?' Prue said tremulously. 'I'd be so grateful. I've been so worried lately, you see. I know what it feels like when you can't sleep. I've got my Finals this year, and Mum's been very ill lately—I've had the worry of that on top of everything else. I try to do my best at work, but sometimes it all gets on top of me . . .'

'I know you do your best,' Trina soothed. 'And your ward is always the neatest in the hospital—everyone says so.'

'Do they?' Prue looked grateful.

'Yes, they do. You're very much appreciated.' There were footsteps and the sound of voices coming up the corridor, and Trina straightened. 'Here come the others. Now cheer up and put it out of your mind. I'll explain to this Dr——?'

'Dr Bayne, I think he's called.'

'To this Dr Bayne for you if I see him this morning. Now here's Sister Price, so you'd better sit up straight and get ready to give us the Report. Don't let her know you've got into a state about it, and I'll have a word with her on the quiet later.'

Prue nodded wanly and straightened her back. 'Thanks, Trina, I—I mean Staff Nurse Morgan. You're so kind.'

At ten-thirteen precisely, Trina was making beds with Pat Raynes, a second-year student, when it happened, and she got her first taste of the dreaded Dr Bayne. Sister Price had gone to coffee when the telephone rang in her office, and Trina went to answer it. As she was the senior on the ward in Sister's absence, this was her responsibility.

As she went in to answer the phone, she realised there was already someone in there. A tall dark man in a white coat was hunched over the desk with his back to her, studying a patient's notes.

Trina had time to do no more than glance at the broad back before she picked up the receiver. 'Merton Ward,' she said. 'Staff Nurse Morgan speaking.'

'Morning, Staff.' Mr Prosser's cultured tones held just a trace of the Italian ancestry he was so proud of. 'I'm sending you up a chap with a query PPU. You've got a bed, I take it?'

'Yes, sir,' answered Trina, glancing at the bed statement lying by the phone. 'We've got two male ones.'

'Jolly good,' the smooth tones replied. 'Let Dr Bayne know when he comes in, will you? Tell him to get in touch with me after he's seen the patient.'

'I will, sir.' Trina glanced at the broad back still turned to her. 'Did you want to speak to him now?'

'Not necessary until he's seen the patient,' the consultant said, and rang off.

Trina turned to the tall figure in the white coat. 'Excuse me,' she said politely, 'I imagine you must be Dr Bayne. Mr Prosser is sending us a man with a query perforated peptic ulcer. He wants you to get in touch with him as soon as you've seen the patient.'

The man turned, and Trina found herself staring up into an unusually arresting face. He had golden skin under curly dark hair, and a pair of the most icy grey eyes she had ever seen.

For a moment he stared at her. Then he spoke, a frown of irritation darkening his face. 'Was that Mr Prosser on the phone?'

Trina nodded. The man's gaze seemed to go right through her, and she forced her voice to stay professional. 'He wants you to ring him as soon as you've seen the patient.'

His frown deepened. 'Why on earth didn't you hand me over to him just now?' he asked abruptly.

She stared back at him, nonplussed. 'I asked if he

wanted to speak to you,' she said, more calmly than she felt. 'But he said it wasn't necessary.'

The man's mouth thinned and he looked her up and down. Trina felt herself blush, and tightened her grip on her composure.

He turned his eyes away, and without further ado picked up the set of notes he had been reading and strode into one of the women's cubicles.

Trina followed him, not quite knowing what else to do. It was standard procedure that a nurse accompanied a doctor whenever he went to examine a patient, and it wasn't too obvious exactly where Dr Bayne was heading. Annoyed at his unreasonable attitude, she could do little else but trail after him.

He halted at one of the beds halfway down the cubicle, peered at his notes and then at the patient's ticket above the bed. 'Mrs Knibb?'

The woman, whose bed had been made, was sitting on the side of it sipping her mid-morning coffee. She had been admitted two days earlier with acute abdominal pain that had been diagnosed as cholecystitis at first, but the pain had subsided after twenty-four hours in hospital and she was now eager to go home. She winked at Trina. 'Hello, love.'

'Hello, Mrs Knibb,' Trina greeted her. 'This is Dr Bayne.' She started to draw the bed-curtains, but Dr Bayne stopped her with a wave of his hand.

'That's not necessary,' he said. 'And I shan't need a chaperone. You can go back to whatever you were doing.'

'I'm sorry,' Trina said steadily, 'but if you're going to examine Mrs Knibb, I have to be present.'

She braced herself for his cutting reply, but he waved

her away as if she were merely an irritation. 'I'm not going to examine her, I'm merely going to ask her a few questions. You can go.'

'All right,' Trina said reluctantly. 'But please call me if you change your mind. It's a rule of this hospital that a nurse is always present when a doctor examines a female patient.'

Mrs Knibb gave her an encouraging nod. 'I'll be all right, dear.'

'I'm sure you will,' Trina said steadily. She turned to Dr Bayne. 'Before I go, is there anything you want?'

He let those grey eyes rest on her. 'Like what, precisely?'

She shrugged. 'A sphygmomanometer? Her chart?'

'I think I can probably find those for myself,' he said, his face suddenly breaking into a smile that was as heartwarming as it was unexpected. 'And if I change my mind about examining her, I promise I'll let you know.'

Thus dismissed, Trina had no option than to leave them. She went back to help Pat Raynes, who was struggling to make beds single-handed, with a most peculiar mixture of exasperation and confusion at the pit of her stomach.

She helped Pat as they worked their way steadily round the three male cubicles, stripping beds neatly, fluffing up the pillows, then remaking the beds again. Well used to the morning routine, they worked steadily on. The beds made, they started the morning treatments, Trina trying hard to ignore the challenging presence of Dr Bayne sitting on the side of Mrs Knibb's bed.

By the time Trina had settled old Mrs Perkins comfortably in her chair with her water jug and glass to hand,

THAT HAUNTING MALADY 19

Dr Bayne had disappeared. Sister Price's large figure appeared in the ward and beckoned to Trina. 'Have you had your coffee yet, Staff?'

'Not yet, Sister.'

'Then you'd better go now, and take Nurse Raynes with you. I take it the beds are all done?'

'Yes, Sister.'

'Good girl! We're in good time this morning. Dr Bayne tells me Mr Prosser is sending in a patient. Is the bed ready for him?'

Trina nodded. 'There's a new set of blank notes on the locker, and I've laid up an IV trolley.'

'Good girl. Off you go now, and take Nurse Raynes with you.'

Walking back from their coffee break in the dining room, Trina and Pat Raynes saw the angular figure of the senior Sister Tutor coming up the corridor towards them.

She was accompanied by two very young student nurses, neither of whom Trina had seen before. One of them was a fresh-faced girl of about eighteen, the other was dark and small-boned, obviously of Indian race. They both looked at Trina, awed.

'Ah, Staff Nurse Morgan!' Miss Hammond's face broke into a smile. 'I was just coming your way. This is Nurse Patel,' she said, introducing the Indian girl, 'and this is Nurse Stevens. They're both in Introductory Block. I wonder if you could take them along to the ward now and introduce them to Sister Price. They're scheduled for your ward this afternoon.'

'Of course, Miss Hammond,' Trina said politely. She smiled at the nervous-looking students.

'Go along with Staff Nurse Morgan now,' Miss Hammond told them both. 'You're both to spend this afternoon on Merton. And don't look like that,' she added to them both with a smile, 'no one's going to eat you!'

The students smiled nervously at Trina and Pat. Miss Hammond's thin figure moved away waving, and the students stared longingly after her.

'Come on,' said Trina briskly. 'We'd better get a move on. Nurse Patel, wasn't it?' she said to the Indian girl, who nodded. Pat Raynes was chatting to Nurse Stevens.

'Did you train in this hospital?' Nurse Patel asked shyly in her excellent English as Trina whisked them along the corridors that led back to Merton Ward.

'Yes, I did,' said Trina, amused. She remembered feeling the same degree of awe towards staff nurses when she herself had been a first-year student only four years before. They had seemed like gods to her then; strange that she was now in that enviable position herself, and well aware that she was only a mere mortal!

Sister Price was in her office when they reached the ward. She looked up as Trina knocked on the door, and stood up to welcome the students.

Trina introduced them. She left them with Sister Prince and went to start the medicine round.

'I'll do the dressings, shall I, Staff?' Pat Raynes was well used to the routine.

'Please,' Trina nodded. 'I'll be with you as soon as I've finished this.'

A little later she saw the students peering into the ward round Sister Price's ample figure, their faces alive with awe and anxiety, and smiled to herself. Poor little kids, it was terrifying to be faced with the prospect of a busy ward when you were so new. Still, they would soon settle in, and after a few weeks it would seem as if they belonged there, even if they did seem to spend the whole of their first six months in the sluice! She chuckled, remembering her own first introduction to bedpans.

She looked up from the medicine trolley at Mr Spinks as he wandered by with a urine bag over one arm. 'All right this morning, Mr Spinks?'

'Fine, thank you, Staff. I'm off to play a hand of whist with the lads in the day room.'

'Good for you,' grinned Trina. 'Have you had your dressing done?'

He nodded. 'Nurse Raynes took my stitches out. She says it's healed a treat.'

'Must be all the fruit your wife keeps bringing you,' Trina told him. 'Keep it up. There's nothing like Vitamin C to speed up the healing process.'

She moved the trolley on round the beds, pausing to hand out tablets and mixtures and exchanging a cheery word with the patients.

She had just finished the medicine round when the new admission arrived with the ambulance men. While Sister Price took his wife into her office, Trina went to assist getting him into bed.

He looked very ill, pale and shocked, sweat beading his brow. She pulled the curtains round the bed and reached over from the far side of it to help move the patient across on the stretcher.

The ambulance men lifted the stretcher on to the bed, pulled out the two long poles, and Trina gently placed the bed-pack of bedclothes on top of the patient. The ambulance men collected their pillows and red blankets and left the ward, waving cheerily to the new patient.

Trina bent over to speak to him. 'Mr Dalby?'

The patient's eyes opened, and focused on her face. He was about fifty but, haggard with pain, appeared a good deal older. His skin was pale and clammy, and when she felt his pulse, Trina could feel the feebleness of the beat and volume, a sure sign of severe shock.

She reached for the sphygmomanometer with which to take his blood pressure, lifting his arm gently to wrap the cuff round his forearm. She attached the lead and began to pump up the cuff.

Mr Dalby watched her listlessly, his eyelids drooping with pain. The mercury slid down the glass tube of the sphyg, and Trina was careful to disguise her anxiety. His blood pressure was very low.

She filled in her observations on the chart. Then the bed curtains were whisked sideways as Dr Bayne came in, followed by Sister Price. Trina silently showed them Mr Dalby's chart.

The Ward Sister nodded, her face careful not to betray any reaction. 'I've just got to pop down to Admin,' she said quietly to Trina, who nodded. 'I'll only be a couple of minutes. I'll leave you with Staff Nurse,' she added to Dr Bayne, who glanced briefly at Trina and then turned back to concentrate on his patient. Sister Price withdrew.

Dr Bayne's examination of the patient was swift and sure. His fingers moving gently over the man's rigid abdomen, he asked questions in a quietly authoritative voice, allaying anxiety and concentrating on the patient's history: asking about his indigestion, his eating habits and whether or not he smoked. Mr Dalby answered as well as he could, and in a short time the examination was over.

Ignoring Trina, Dr Bayne concluded his examination and stood up. Mr Dalby's eyes followed him anxiously. 'What do you think it is, doctor?'

'Well, old chap,' Dr Bayne said gently, 'it looks as if you've got a bit of an ulcer in your stomach, and we think it's probably perforated. I'm afraid it means an operation.'

Mr Dalby nodded. 'Anything, doctor. I just want to get well again. Can you fix it?'

'You bet we can!' Dr Bayne's voice was reassuring. 'But I'm afraid we'll have to operate right away. What did you have for breakfast?'

Mr Dalby shook his head weakly. 'Didn't have any.'

'Anything to drink?'

'Nothing.'

Dr Bayne nodded. 'Good. We'll have you in theatre in about twenty minutes. All right?'

The patient's eyes closed and he nodded gratefully. Dr Bayne strode out through the curtains and back towards the office.

Trina quickly collected the things she needed to get Mr Dalby ready for theatre. She attached an identity band round his wrist with his name, date of birth, consultant and ward, and dressed him quickly and gently in operation gown, theatre socks and cap, checking for false teeth and making sure his wrist watch was removed.

She went into Sister Price's office and locked Mr Dalby's watch in the ward safe. Dr Bayne was in there, talking to the patient's wife.

'It means an operation, an emergency one,' he was saying as she went in. 'Sorry there's no other way.'

'That's all right, doctor,' Mrs Dalby said gratefully,

'We understand.' She stood up.

Trina handed Mr Dalby's treatment sheet to Dr Bayne. 'Stay with your husband for the moment,' she told Mrs Dalby as she left the office. 'We'll be back in a tick to give him an injection to help him get to sleep.' She followed the woman out of the office. 'Don't worry, he'll be in good hands.'

Mrs Dalby smiled tearfully. 'Thank you, nurse. You're all so kind.'

Trina glanced quickly round the ward. The auxiliaries were still giving out the mid-morning drinks from their trolley. She quickly hooked a NIL BY MOUTH notice above Mr Dalby's bed, then went back into the office.

Inside, Dr Bayne was sitting at Sister Price's desk writing up his notes. He reached for the treatment sheet as Trina came in, then carried on writing, taking no notice of her.

'Excuse me,' Trina said formally.

He looked up, plainly irritated.

She refused to be dismayed. 'I'm sorry to interrupt,' she said, 'but do you want us to pass a Ryles tube before he goes to theatre? And what about a drip?'

He waved her away. 'We'll do all that down there,' he said, as if she were an irritating child, 'there's no time now. I want him dressed and ready in five minutes. Understood?'

Trina nodded. 'Actually, he's already prepared.'

He looked surprised. 'Is he?'

'Yes,' she said calmly. 'And what about a pre-med, or will you give him that in theatre too?'

His eyes flickered over her. 'No, I'll write him up for something now,' he said, writing rapidly on the prescription sheet.

Trina waited until he had finished. She took the sheet from his outstretched hand and glanced at it. 'Oh, and Dr Bayne,' she said politely, 'while you're here, I wonder if I could have a word with you. It's about last night.' She paused. 'I believe the night nurse on this ward, Nurse Gant, phoned you about——'

The grey eyes regarded her. 'Ah yes, the inefficient twit who called me out at three o'clock in the morning.'

'That's hardly fair,' Trina said levelly. 'Nurse Gant is not an inefficient twit. She happens to be a particularly anxious student nurse who——'

He interrupted her, fixing her with a steely eye. 'Look,' he said coldly, 'I would be more than happy to discuss the characters and shortcomings of nurses with you if we were off duty, but right now I'm more than a little concerned that Mr Dalby gets to the operating theatre in the next few minutes. I would appreciate it if we could have this stimulating debate at some other time. Do you mind?'

Trina felt her face grow furiously red. She could have kicked herself. He was absolutely right! How could she have been so incredibly stupid as to try and tackle him about Prue at such an inappropriate moment? She must need her head examined! 'I'm terribly sorry!' she gasped, and promptly fled, aghast at her own stupidity.

As she ran from the office she was aware of Dr Bayne picking up the telephone receiver and calmly asking the switchboard for Mr Prosser.

Escorting Mr Dalby along the corridors on a trolley with the theatre porters twenty minutes later, Trina had recovered her composure a little. Mr Dalby was dozing, the premedication having taken effect, but his face was still ashen with shock.

Pausing at the main Theatre doors, Trina paused to change into white rubber theatre boots. The double doors swung open to admit them, and she squeezed Mr Dalby's hand. 'Here's the operating theatre, Mr Dalby,' she told him gently. 'They'll soon fix you up in here.'

'Thank you, nurse.' Mr Dalby's face tightened in a spasm of pain.

As Trina handed his notes with the prescription sheet clipped uppermost to the assistant anaesthetist, she could see into the scrub room, where Dr Bayne was standing at the sink in his vest and operating trousers, scrubbing briskly and methodically at his arms from elbows to fingertips. He was deeply engrossed in conversation with Mr Prosser, who was standing next to him similarly attired, and scrubbing away too.

She looked away hastily and concentrated on what she was there to do. As she gently and deftly exchanged his ward pillows for the theatre's own thinner one, Mr Dalby opened his eyes and gave her a feeble smile.

'Off you go to sleep,' she told him, patting his hand as Dr Duncan, the anaesthetist, approached. 'We'll see you when you get back to the ward.'

Sarah Wade, the theatre staff nurse and Trina's second flatmate, came over to them and smiled at the patient. 'Mr Bernard Dalby?'

Trina and the patient both nodded. The girls were fairly formal in a patient's hearing, as was appropriate on duty.

Sarah bent to check Mr Dalby's wristband and compare it with his notes. 'What do you think of Mr Prosser's new houseman?' she whispered aside to Trina when she had satisfied herself that the information matched.

Trina made a face. 'Not a lot. A bit of an ogre, isn't he?'

Sarah looked surprised. 'Oh? We think he's rather dishy. He's good, too. Did an emergency appendix from Kids' ward last night that was very nasty, and made a super job of it too. His wife's lovely, a gorgeous redhead—have you seen her?'

The anaesthetist turned to ask Sarah to hold up the patient's chin prior to intubation, and Sarah winked. This was Trina's signal to withdraw from the anaesthetic room, and she did so, with a last reassuring smile at Mr Dalby.

We think he's rather dishy. The words echoed in her ears as she changed back into her shoes outside the main theatre doors. Not my cup of tea, thanks, she thought grimly as she placed the ward pillows on the shelf provided for the purpose, labelled them with a paper towel and pinned it to the topmost pillow.

And as she retraced her steps quickly to the ward through corridors fragrant with the smell of shepherd's pie being prepared for the patients' lunches, she followed that up mentally with, 'Hmm, well, I hope he's a lot more considerate to his wife than he was to poor Prue Gant.' Dr Bayne dishy? He could go and take a running jump, for all she cared. So then why did the memory of him standing at the theatre sink in his vest and operating trousers disturb her so?

She pushed the ward doors open crossly. Married or not, the man was already invading her thoughts far too much. I suppose I'll get used to him, she thought heavily. After all, I'm going to have to work with him for the next six months. The fact that I find him objectionable isn't going to make one jot of difference to the way I treat him on duty. I shall be calm and coolly efficient—and completely detached. And if our paths cross off duty —well, he's married, so that's not likely to happen.

Off duty—that reminded her of this evening. Alan! She thought, her heart sinking. Now what on earth am I going to do about Alan?

CHAPTER TWO

COMING off duty that evening at a little after five, Trina made for the changing room with a sigh of relief. She adored her job, but it was always a special pleasure to leave the ward after a tiring day, knowing that she had earned her evening's recreation. She had spent the afternoon with the two new student nurses trailing after her, showing them how to take blood pressures and record observations in between all her usual routine work. And this evening there was the problem of Alan to tackle. She had got to do something about Alan.

She sighed, shelving the problem temporarily while she thought back over the afternoon. Mr Dalby had come back from Theatre with an IVI in situ after a partial gastrectomy, and this had meant sitting him up as soon as his blood pressure had stabilised, and aspirating his Ryles tube at regular intervals to make sure the suture line in his stomach was kept dry. Fortunately she had not come into contact with Dr Bayne again, and she felt relieved. At least she had been able to concentrate on her work, knowing that he was probably still operating; Mr Prosser's list often went on well after five o'clock.

Trina sighed again, cross now that she had allowed herself to get so nettled during the morning. She thought about the situation objectively. Dr Bayne had probably been tired from lack of sleep during the Prue Gant episode last night, and that was why he had been so irritable.

She bit her lip, wishing she had had an opportunity to explain Prue's side of it fully. Ah well, it was too late now. She could hardly make a special point of contacting him to go into further details over it! Prue would just have to sort it out on her own.

She rounded a bend in the corridor on her way to the changing room, glanced absently through a window that faced the car park, and was surprised to see a low-slung sports car pulling in to one of the spaces reserved for the doctors. The car slid smoothly to a stop and a leggy redhead wearing an attractive coat swung long legs out of it, then stood up. She stood beside the car looking round for a moment as if unsure, then made her way towards the gatekeeper's little booth.

Bill, the attendant on duty, could be seen approaching her; they met halfway across the park. The redhead said something, pointed to the car, and Bill nodded. Then, to Trina's surprise, he made his way happily back to the booth, and the girl turned and made her way across the tarmac towards the residency flats.

Trina shrugged and turned away from the window. So that was Dr Bayne's wife. Well, he certainly had good taste. The girl looked about twenty-four, and wore her shoulder-length red hair tossed back with artless ease. Trina sneaked another look. The girl wore expensive-looking high-heeled boots and dark green corduroy jeans, and was muffled against the February wind in a fashionable rabbitskin coat. As Trina watched, she ran lightly up the steps of the Residency flats towards the swing doors, and disappeared inside.

Trina continued on towards the changing room, her heart inexplicably heavy. Ah well, another day over.

Her feet ached, and the thought of a long hot bath beckoned.

Reaching the front door of the flat ten minutes later, she rummaged in her handbag for the key and let herself into the hallway of the Victorian house. Their flat was on the top floor, and underneath them lived an Indian family of mother, father and three sons. The tantalising smell of Indian cooking floated into the narrow hall.

Damn! thought Trina, thinking of their own planned supper. She had forgotten the eggs. She looked at her watch; it was twenty past five. If she hurried, she would just be able to catch the corner shop, which closed at five-thirty.

The door of the downstairs flat opened and Mrs Patel peeped round it, obviously expecting one of her family home. The delicious smell grew stronger. Her face broke into a nervous smile when she saw Trina.

'Hello, Mrs Patel!' Trina called breezily. 'You're having curry for supper! I can smell it.'

Mrs Patel nodded, then shook her head. Her English was not very good, and she was often nervous about it. 'Not curry,' she said carefully. 'We are having one of my recipes, *rogan josh*.'

'What's that?' asked Trina. 'It smells heavenly.'

'I will give recipe,' the woman said eagerly, 'if you like.'

'Please!' Trina smiled. 'I'd love to try it. Your meals always smell delicious. Look, I must fly—I've got to catch the corner shop. Is there anything you need?'

Mrs Patel shook her head and withdrew with another shy smile.

Trina hurried down the road. The corner shop was in the process of closing and she dashed inside just in the nick of time. Grabbing a wire basket, she headed for where the eggs were kept. She put two half-dozen boxes of the largest ones into her basket, added a loaf of wholemeal bread en route for the till, then to her horror she saw that Dr Bayne of all people was standing just beyond the till, peering at the biscuit stand! He had a wrapped bottle of something in his hand, and a loaf the same as hers. Before Trina could think of dodging back behind a stand to avoid him, he turned enquiringly and saw her.

For a moment he stared as if puzzled, then his face cleared. 'Well, if it isn't little Nurse Joan of Arc,' he said pleasantly. 'From Merton Ward, isn't it? I didn't recognise you at first without your armour.'

'Good evening, Dr Bayne,' said Trina, as sweetly as she could manage. 'And it's *Staff* Nurse, not Nurse.'

He raised his eyebrows, and gave her a little bow. 'I beg your pardon, *Staff* Nurse Joan of Arc.'

There was a pointed cough from the shopkeeper waiting at the till, and Dr Bayne waved a hand. To Trina's relief, he called his thanks and left the shop with his purchases, closing the door behind him.

'Who's he?' the shopkeeper asked with interest, jerking his head towards the door. 'Never seen him before. New bloke, is he?'

'Mr Prosser's new houseman,' Trina told him with a sigh. 'Thank goodness he's gone.' Without his presence, at least she could concentrate on what she was doing.

'Don't you like him?' the shopkeeper asked as she paid for her purchases. 'Looks nice enough to me.'

'I hardly know him,' Trina said shortly. 'Have you got a carrier bag, please?'

Leaving the shop, she was horrified to realise Dr

Bayne was waiting for her outside. He smiled as Trina approached him, which she couldn't fail to do given where he was standing on the pavement, without being deliberately rude. They fell into step together.

Trina decided that social niceties could be dispensed with. 'Why did you wait for me?' she asked coolly. 'We don't know each other, do we?'

'I could hardly do otherwise,' he answered with a wry grin. 'After all, we are colleagues, professionally speaking. How's Mr Dalby this afternoon?'

'He's fine,' said Trina, annoyed that she couldn't walk home alone and think her own thoughts about Dr Bayne rather than having his presence thrust upon her. 'I'd have called you if he wasn't, wouldn't I?' That sounded ungracious, so she added quickly, 'Look, I'm sorry I tried to tackle you about Nurse Gant this morning. I chose a very inopportune time.'

'That's all right,' he said easily. 'I admire your flying to the defence of your nurses. Think nothing of it.'

'All the same,' she went on, 'she is in a nervous state at the moment. Her mother——'

'Look,' he said, stopping and turning towards her, 'the domestic problems of nurses are no concern of mine. As far as I'm concerned, by the time I got to the ward the patient in question was fast asleep and snoring. It was quite unnecessary to call me.'

'I realise that,' Trina said levelly, 'but was it necessary to upset my nurse in quite so acid a manner? All that was needed was a quiet reassurance that you would change the sedation in the morning. It was most unkind to be so cutting—Nurse Gant was only doing her best.'

He fixed her with a steely eye. 'Staff Nurse,' he said coldly, 'if you had been operating until one-thirty after a long day and then fallen asleep at two, would you have been quite so rational if wakened an hour later by a wet request for something so trivial as a change of night sedation? I rather doubt it.'

'I might have attempted to be a little more understanding,' Trina retorted. 'Nurse Gant only had the patient's interest at heart.'

'But not the doctor's?'

'No, definitely not the doctor's. A doctor is there to be called if a nurse is worried. Nurse Gant *was* worried. That's why she called you.'

He looked her up and down, his eyes as icy as the February pavements. 'I can see,' he said slowly, 'that compassion is not a quality you yourself hold in much regard.'

Trina's cheeks were flaming. 'Oh yes, I do!' she flared. 'But my compassion is strictly for my patients and my nurses, and not at all for the medical staff who, I'm sure, get all the compassion they need from other sources.'

His grey eyes were steely. 'Oh? Such as whom?'

'Such as——' Trina faltered. 'Such as—your wife,' she finished furiously.

He looked slightly blank. 'My wife?'

'Yes, your wife,' she repeated. 'Apparently you have one.'

His face cleared. 'Ah, I see. Hospital gossip has been busy already.' He looked faintly amused. 'There's no escape from it, is there? Ah well,' he said as they carried on walking, 'no great harm done, other than to my chronic lack of sleep. Would it help if I apologised to this Nurse Gant of yours next time I see her?'

Trina was taken aback. 'Would you?'

He nodded. 'I might consider it.'

The arrogance of the man! she fumed inwardly. Aloud she said, 'It might help her confidence a bit if you did. She's not very sure of herself, really.' That sounded rather meaningless, so she added, 'I mean, she's very worried about her mother, so . . .' She was floundering, and her words trailed off.

'I understand,' he said. 'Let's forget it, shall we? What are you doing tonight?'

Trina blinked. 'What?'

'I asked what you were doing tonight. Are you busy?'

He's a married man, Trina thought, aghast, and he's about to ask me for a date! She stopped in her tracks and turned to him. 'I'm sorry, Dr Bayne,' she said stiffly, 'but I don't go out with married men.'

The ghost of a smile lurked at the corners of his mouth. 'Married men?'

'Yes,' she said. 'I don't go out with married men.'

'Very wise of you, I'm sure,' he replied wryly. 'Oh, I see! You assumed that I was asking you out. Actually, I wasn't. I was merely enquiring, in the interests of conversation, whether you were doing anything tonight. I wasn't aware that I was asking you for a date.'

Trina felt utterly mortified. She could have died of embarrassment. She felt herself grow hot and cold. 'I'm sorry,' she managed to stammer, 'I thought you were.'

'Well, you were wrong.' He paused. 'As a matter of fact, I *am* off duty this evening, but I'm afraid I have something planned.' He held up the bottle.

To Trina's everlasting relief they had reached the flat by now, and she paused thankfully. Any minute now and she would be free of him.

A window opened above them and Mandy stuck her head out. She called down breezily. 'Trina? Did you get the eggs?' She waved and withdrew, closing the window again.

Dr Bayne smiled to himself. 'So—Staff Nurse Joan of Arc has a name. Trina? Hmm, rather coy, isn't it? Somehow I'd imagined you'd be called something warlike. Boadicea or Brunnhilde would suit you much better. Well, since I now know your name, you'd better know mine, hadn't you?'

'Your name? But I know your name. It's Dr Bayne.'

His eyes held hers. 'I mean my christian name.'

Trina could have kicked herself. Why did she have to become so stupid when she was in his presence? 'I'm sorry,' she said, 'I wasn't thinking. Of course you must have a christian name.'

'It's Giles,' Dr Bayne said wryly. Then he turned on his heel and left her standing there on the step.

Keith had already arrived when Trina went into the flat. He and Mandy were sitting entwined together on the sofa, watching TV. Mandy grinned when Trina came in. 'Who was that gorgeous man you were talking to outside?'

Trina grimaced. 'That was Mr Prosser's new houseman, the famous Dr Bayne. Gorgeous he may be, but he's also married, and very, very slippery.'

'At least you got the eggs,' Mandy observed. 'Look, Keith, you'll be eating tonight after all. Go and have your bath, Trina. The water's all ready and you're keeping this man from his food. I do hope Alan won't be long—I'm starving!'

Trina handed over the eggs, collected her clothes and her portable radio, and ran herself a deep bath. Soaking in the scented suds, she let the long day fall away from her. How good it was to do a satisfying job and lie in luxury at the end of it! Music would make it perfect.

She reached out a hand and turned the dial to Radio Two, leaning back to listen to a girl's voice singing a wistful song about lost love. *No cure for love, that haunting malady*, went the words. The soapy water was soothingly delicious, the girl's voice gentle and assured, and Trina nearly feel asleep.

She was roused by the sound of the doorbell, and started to soap herself hurriedly.

'Hurry up in there!' Mandy rapped on the bathroom door. 'Alan's here and he's as hungry as we are, so I'm starting your omelette now. This is going to be an experience you'll never forget!'

'I'm coming!' called Trina. She listened to the last sad strains of the girl's voice on the radio as the song faded out on a high note. The tune was oddly haunting, and she only just caught the name of it as the DJ sighed mock-wistfully and said, '*That Haunting Malady*. Ah, such a sad lady! Never mind, me dears, here's the latest from Elton John to cheer you up . . .'

Trina turned the radio off and concentrated on drying and dressing quickly. The song had left her with an ache somewhere in the region of her heart that reminded her, for some strange reason, of Mr Dalby. Or was it that awful Dr Bayne? She simply must get a grip on herself, she thought firmly. Why should she find his personality so objectionable that he addled her wits the way he did? It was ridiculous in a grown woman of twenty-two.

She pulled clean jeans on to her slim hips and struggled into a warm polo-necked jumper. Thank goodness she could wear comfortable clothes this evening; it wasn't necessary to dress up for Alan. She sighed.

What was she going to do about Alan? Should she warn him that it was pointless for him to go on assuming their relationship was anything more than friendship? Did he assume that it was anyway? She and Alan had never been more than friends. Good friends, to be sure—but there had never been anything more than that on Trina's side. What about Alan?

Emerging from the steamy bathroom into the garlic-scented kitchen, Trina saw an opened bottle of wine on the table, and realised that Alan must have brought it. She poured herself a glass, then took it into the sitting room to find them all in there tucking into Mandy's huge omelettes with bread and butter.

'Yours is in the oven,' Mandy told her, waving a fork. 'I haven't put garlic in because I know you don't like it, so if the rest of us reek to high heaven you'll have to put up with it.'

Not that it matters much, thought Trina, retrieving her omelette from the oven where it was keeping warm, Alan and I have never been close enough to let a little thing like garlic come between us! She put her plate on to a tray and took it in to the others.

The omelette was delicious. So was Alan's wine. They all sat round eating, enjoying each other's easy company.

'I nearly phoned you to put you off this evening,' Trina confessed to Alan as she sat beside him on the sofa. 'I was afraid I wouldn't be much company tonight, it's been a hectic day on the ward.'

'You should have done,' Alan said easily. 'I'd have understood.' Dear old Alan, he always did understand. He was looking unusually nice this evening, and Trina wondered for at least the hundredth time why he didn't set her heart on fire in the prescribed manner. 'I wouldn't have minded, honestly,' he went on. 'I know how shattered you get after a full day.'

She dug her fork into her omelette. It was cooked with herbs and filled with mushrooms, which oozed thickly out of the inside. 'What sort of a day have you had?' she asked Alan, as she ate.

He shrugged. 'Same old boring routine. Just a load of old figures, I'm afraid—nothing heroic like saving lives like you lot.'

Trina looked at him, remembering. Two years ago when she had been a second-year student nurse, Alan had come in to hospital to have his appendix out. He had asked her out when he'd been discharged. She had always liked him; he was easy-going, considerate and kind. His work as a chartered accountant meant that he was always free in the evenings, and he had been patient with Trina's often awkward hours off duty. Glad to have someone to be good friends with outside the hospital, she had encouraged his interest, even though Alan probably realised she didn't return it with anything more than friendship. He was definitely the marrying kind; he wanted nothing more than a wife and a home with children, he had made no secret of that. But had he got ambitions towards Trina?

She finished her omelette and put the plate down, glancing at him. He was watching Mandy and Keith thoughtfully, perhaps envious of their easy affection with each other. She wondered whether it was fair to him to let things go on as they were. Perhaps she ought to make it clear to him exactly how she felt?

'You know,' Keith said casually at last, laying his plate aside and looking at Mandy, 'I think we ought to start thinking about getting married.' He winked across the room towards Trina and Alan. 'Any woman who can cook like you do should be snapped up quick—don't you agree, Alan?'

'Oh, I do,' grinned Alan. 'Why don't you ask her properly?'

Mandy, who was sitting at Keith's feet wiping a crust of bread round her plate, looked up quickly.

'How do you feel about it?' Keith asked her. 'Be careful what you say—I've got witnesses, don't forget.' He winked at them again.

'I thought you'd never ask,' laughed Mandy, although her eyes were dancing. 'You name the day, and I'll oblige by turning up in a wedding dress with a bunch of roses. You've only got to say when.'

'All right,' said Keith. 'How about April?'

She put her head on one side. 'Depends on the weather. And, of course, whether I'm on duty or not.' She looked thoughtful. 'Church or register office?'

'Oh, church, of course,' said Keith. 'Nothing but the best for us.' His eyes grew serious. 'I mean it, Mandy. Will you marry me this April?'

The room grew quiet. Trina held her breath.

Mandy turned her face to Keith. 'Seriously?' she asked.

He nodded. 'Seriously. I've been wanting to ask you for a long time now. Somehow it's easier in company.'

Mandy had leapt to her feet with a shriek of joy. She flung her arms round Keith's neck. 'Do you really mean it? Really and truly?'

'Really and truly,' he told her, kissing her warmly on the lips. 'We can get engaged tomorrow if you like—buy a ring and all that to make it official. That is, if you say yes.'

'Oh, yes! Yes! Yes!' Mandy was beside herself with joy. 'Oh, how lovely! Keith, I thought you'd never ask!' She was nearly in tears. She sat on Keith's knee and hugged him rapturously, smothering his face with kisses.

'Come on, Trina,' said Alan, getting to his feet and collecting their plates. 'Let's go and wash up, leave these two lovebirds to have a private moment together.'

'Oh, blow the washing up!' Mandy's eyes danced. 'Who cares about boring things like that at a time like this? I want to celebrate! Oh, Keith darling, do you really, *really* mean it?'

'I certainly do,' Keith told her. 'Tell you what, why don't we all go down to the Can for a drink to celebrate and I'll treat you all. Just to prove I'm serious,' he added to Mandy, depositing a kiss on the end of her nose. 'How about it, eh?'

'Terrific!' went the general chorus. The King Canute was their local pub, a gathering place for off-duty hospital staff, and known affectionately as the Can. It was warm and cosy and a welcome haven on chilly evenings, especially so when the male nurses were there with their instruments. Two of them played guitars and one a banjo, and their combined sound was surprisingly professional.

The band were playing tonight. As the four young people entered the warm atmosphere they could hear the familiar strains coming from the lounge bar. The boys had a standing arrangement with the landlord: in exchange for their music he provided them with free beer. The sound was good, and attracted quite a few extra people into the pub, drawn by the novelty of live music.

Alan, Mandy and Trina sat down at Keith's insistence. He took their orders and went to wait at the bar to be served. While he was gone the band tuned their instruments again and then struck up a rollicking chorus of *Show Me The Way To Go Home*. Well oiled by their free beer, they played with gusto, and the bar grew warmer and cosier by the minute, seeming far away from the icy February weather outside.

Keith came back to them with the drinks, then sat down next to Mandy. They toasted each other, Trina and Alan joining in, then they all sat listening to the band, tapping their feet in time with the music and exchanging talk and casual hospital gossip. The atmosphere was relaxed and friendly, and the ward seemed far away.

'Are you all right?' Trina whispered to Alan during a lull in the music. He seemed rather subdued. 'You seem a bit down this evening.'

Alan smiled to himself. 'Yes, I'm all right,' he said wanly.

'You're not all right,' she told him. 'Now come on, tell me the truth. What's getting you down?'

He sighed. 'Everything and nothing, really. Oh, I don't know, it all seems a bit pointless sometimes, that's all. Doesn't it to you?'

Trina considered this. 'I know what you mean,' she sympathised. 'We all get like that sometimes. The trouble with you, Alan, is that you ought to be married. That's what's wrong with you—you need a wife. Someone to love.'

He nodded, and smiled feebly to himself.

'You know it's no good asking me, don't you,' Trina said bravely, determined to put him in the clear as far as her own feelings were concerned. 'I'm not your type, am I?'

He shrugged listlessly. 'Would you marry me if I asked you?' he said, looking up at her.

'No, I wouldn't,' she said gently. 'We'd never get on. You're much too well organised for me—in that we're far too alike. Besides, I don't love you, and I don't think you're in love with me either.'

'No, I suppose not,' he confessed. He looked wistful. 'It's rather a pity, isn't it? We make such a good team otherwise.'

'Yes, we do,' Trina agreed. 'But marriage has to be based on something much more than teamwork—for me, anyway.' She paused. 'Do you think we ought to stop seeing each other?'

He looked so mournful that she reached for his hand and held it in hers. It was extraordinary that she could do that with such ease and yet feel nothing more than warm friendship for him.

'Do you want to stop seeing me?' asked Alan.

'Not at all,' Trina told him. 'Unless it makes you unhappy. And so long as we both understand we're perfectly free. The last thing I would want is for you to imagine you owe me some sort of debt. If ever you found somebody else and fell in love, you could drop me immediately. Understood?'

He squeezed her hand. 'But will that ever happen?'

'Of course it will,' Trina told him warmly. She detached her hand to join in the round of applause as the music came to a flourishing close. Looking round the warm room, she suddenly realised that Giles Bayne and his wife were sitting in the corner over to the left of them and beyond the band. She had been so engrossed in conversation with Alan that she hadn't seen them come in. Giles Bayne was looking straight across at her, an inscrutable expression on his face. How long had he been there? Trina had no way of knowing.

Feeling her cheeks redden, she looked away. When she looked back again he was deeply involved in conversation with the redheaded girl beside him, who was smiling at something he was saying. It was difficult to see clearly across the smoky haze, but the girl looked even lovelier than Trina had expected. She was wearing the same green corduroy jeans with a fluffy white sweater on top, and the clothes did nothing to disguise a superb figure.

Trina turned her eyes away quickly, but not before Mandy had followed her gaze. She nudged Trina. 'Look over there,' she whispered, 'that's the guy you were talking to outside the flat, isn't it? Mr Prosser's new houseman, didn't you say he was?'

'Don't look at him,' Trina whispered back imploringly, desperate not to encourage Mandy's interest in the couple. 'I'd rather forget him this evening—I've had more than enough of him already today. Please!' she added urgently.

Mandy sat back. 'Sorry—don't want to embarrass you.'

'I wonder if the band are going to play again,' Trina said desperately, trying to change the subject. She was unnervingly conscious of the couple opposite, and found it difficult to avoid looking in their direction. To her dismay, Dr Bayne was getting to his feet. She prayed that he wasn't going to come over to them.

He wasn't. He went over to the bar and stood there, waiting to order more drinks. His redheaded wife watched him go. She looked oddly sad.

Trina dared to raise her eyes and look towards the bar. Giles Bayne's dark head was turned away from her as he spoke to the barman, and she studied the back of his neck. The curly hair grew thick and low, giving her the ridiculous feeling of longing to feel it with her fingers. This is insane! She told herself angrily. Whatever's the matter with you? He's a married man!

Winding his way back from the bar with a pint of Guinness in one hand and a glass of wine in the other, to Trina's dismay Giles Bayne paused at their table. 'Ah, Staff Nurse Brunnhilde!' he said smoothly, inclining his head to Trina so that she blushed furiously. 'Now I see why you wouldn't come out with me this evening—you were genuinely busy!'

Trina stared at him, nonplussed. 'But—but——' she gasped helplessly. After all he'd said as they'd walked back from the shop together! Speechless with indignation, she stared after him as he gave her a little mock bow and returned with the drinks to his wife.

Trina sank back into her corner seat, confused and angry.

'Did he really ask you out?' Mandy asked her in an awed voice. 'Crikey, what a super bloke! You didn't tell me how good-looking he was close up.'

'Ask me out?' echoed Trina. 'No, he didn't! At least —*if* he did, which I'm not sure, I refused anyway. I told him I don't go out with married men.'

'Is he married?'

'Yes. That's his wife over there with him. The redhead next to him.'

Mandy peered across the room. Trina, glancing covertly after her, saw Giles Bayne raise his glass at them with what could only be described as a smirk.

She looked away quickly. Confused and cross, she stared determinedly in the opposite direction.

'That's funny.' Mandy looked puzzled. 'I seem to know that girl from somewhere—the redhead. She looks sort of familiar.' She frowned thoughtfully.

'Who are they, anyway?' Alan wanted to know. He had followed all this with interest, and glanced across at the couple.

'He's a new doctor,' Mandy told him. 'I don't think Trina thinks much of him. She told me earlier that he was the most awful man she'd come across. Dangerous talk, dear,' she added mischievously to Trina. 'If a man gets under your skin that badly it usually means you'll end up falling in love with him.'

'Not me!' Trina said vehemently. 'And anyway, I——'

'Yes, we know,' said Mandy with a grin, 'you don't go out with married men. Are you absolutely sure he's married?'

'Of course I'm sure!' said Trina, irritated. 'Sarah told me! And even if he's only living with her, I'd still say the same. I do have——'

But before she could say any more, to everyone's surprise Rod Simon, one of the male nurses in the band, put down his guitar and got to his feet. He turned to exchange a whispered word with the other two, who nodded eagerly, then turned to address the audience sitting round him.

'Ladies and gentlemen,' he said importantly, clearing his throat, 'may I have your attention for a moment, please?'

Everyone's eyes turned to him. A hush fell on the assembly. 'You may or may not realise,' Rod went on, 'but this evening we have here with us someone who is rapidly making a name for herself in the world of pop music.' He paused impressively. 'Currently starring in the pantomime *Sleeping Beauty* at the Royal Theatre here in Norchester . . . Ladies and gentlemen,' he held out his hand, 'I am honoured to introduce to you . . . Beth Garland!'

All eyes swung round to where he indicated, and a tide of applause rang round the crowded room. To Trina's amazement, all eyes were focused on Giles Bayne's wife!

Blushing, the redhead got to her feet, gave them all a shy little wave, then sat down again.

'Oh no, you don't!' said Rod, and everybody laughed, 'You don't get off that lightly. We'd be more than honoured if you would sing for us—would you?'

Giles Bayne's wife was *Beth Garland*? Trina was staggered. She had certainly heard the name before.

Mandy grabbed her arm. 'I knew it!' she said excitedly, 'I knew I'd seen her somewhere. Of course, it's Beth Garland! Oh, Trina, she's terrific! I do hope she sings!'

'Would you?' Rod was imploring across the sea of faces.

Beth Garland nodded and stood up again. Applause followed her as she wound her way through the audience and approached the band. Turning to the boys, she had a whispered word with them for a few seconds, the boys nodded eagerly together, then Beth turned back to face her audience, flushing with pleasure.

'Thank you,' she said. Her voice was sweet and low, and everybody clapped again. 'We've decided that the lads here can manage my latest song,' she turned to the band with a smile which was met by more eager nods, 'which I'd like to sing for you now. It's a love song, but rather a sad one, I'm afraid. It means a lot to me personally, and—and I'd like to sing it for you. It's called *That Haunting Malady*.'

The hush in the room fell to nothing. The boys introduced a gentle chord or two on guitars, and Beth began to sing.

Her voice rose and fell in an ache of sound, and Trina listened, spellbound. It was the same song she had heard on the radio while she was in the bath. The melody was pure and sweet, regret for lost love throbbing through the music in Beth's mellow voice. The boys accompanied her very gently on their guitars, a different backing from the record Trina had heard in the bath, but one that suited the song well and gave it an even more wistful air.

> 'No cure for love,
> That haunting malady——
> No treatment in the world
> Could ever set me free——
> No touch but yours can heal,
> No other arms can set me free——
> Because I'm just a hopeless case
> Of that haunting malady . . .'

Trina, listening with an ache in her heart to Beth's voice rising and falling, found herself looking across the room towards Giles Bayne. He was watching his wife with pride, she thought. Suddenly he turned his head and looked directly at her. His gaze was steady and penetrating, as if seeking her out above all others. Trina looked away hastily.

She directed her attention to Alan. He was gazing at Beth with rapture, as if he had never heard anything so lovely in his life. Poor Alan, Trina thought with sudden compassion.

The song drew to a close on a steady high note. For a moment there was a spellbound silence, then a storm of applause thundered round the room. Beth Garland smiled, gave her audience a little wave, then stepped down to make her way back towards Giles. The band raised their hands to her as they clapped, obviously thrilled at having had the chance to accompany a professional singer of such standing.

Trina clapped until her hands ached. At last the applause subsided, the band broke into a rollicking instrumental, and the atmosphere in the pub returned to normal. Mandy could hardly contain her excitement. 'How about that, then!' she said eagerly. 'I knew I'd seen her somewhere before, I just knew it! Gosh, she's super, isn't she? Oh what a fabulous evening!'

Trina peeped across the room to where Beth had returned to Giles Bayne. She saw him pick up the girl's hand and grasp it, and she looked back at him gratefully and adoringly.

Trina turned to Alan. He hadn't said a word since Beth had finished her song. 'What did you think of her? Wasn't she great?'

Before he could answer, Mandy dug Trina in the ribs. 'They're leaving.' She nodded towards the far side of the room. Giles and Beth had got to their feet and were winding their way out between the seated people. Beth gave the band a final wave of her hand, then they were gone.

Trina watched them depart, an ache dragging at her heart. She wasn't entirely sure whether it was for Alan or for herself.

CHAPTER THREE

MANDY woke Trina at seven next morning, bearing a cup of tea. 'Come on!' she called breezily, yanking back Trina's curtains to reveal the icy February morning outside. 'Up you get! It's high time you were awake!'

'Whatever for?' groaned Trina, struggling to sit up. Mandy was a cheerful sight, her plump cheeks flushed with excitement, but Trina would much rather have stayed asleep for another hour or two. She yawned.

'You'll be late! Oh, wasn't it a wonderful evening last night!' Mandy enthused. 'I can't believe it—Beth Garland singing to us live like that! Wasn't it one of the greatest thrills of your life?'

'Very much so,' Trina agreed drily. 'But why wake me up at this horrible hour to remind me, when I'm not on duty until one?'

'Oh, aren't you?' Mandy looked blank. 'I thought I was doing you a favour. I thought you'd forgotten to set your alarm.'

'No, I didn't. I've got a one-to-eight shift today.'

'I'm sorry.' Mandy looked contrite, but it didn't last long. 'I'm far too excited to think straight. Imagine Keith asking me to marry him too! Oh, Trina, I feel as if I'm walking on air!'

'You will be, if you carry on bouncing about all over my tea,' Trina observed. 'Do shut up and sit still for a minute—I've hardly gathered my wits together yet.'

'Sorry,' laughed Mandy. 'But honestly, if you'd just

got engaged to be married you'd know how I feel. Thank goodness I'm nights off. I'm meeting Keith at lunch time to go and choose the ring. Oh, Trina, isn't he wonderful!'

'Delightful,' Trina agreed. 'I hope you'll both be very happy. Where's Sarah?'

'She was called out in the night for a section,' Mandy told her. 'Thank goodness I don't work in Theatre—I like to know that I can call my nights off my own. By the way, there's a bit in the local paper about Beth Garland. Here—read it!'

She shoved the paper at Trina, then went off humming in the direction of the kitchen. Trina heard her clattering plates, then smelled the tantalising aroma of frying bacon. She sipped her tea and leafed through the newspaper, conscious of a heaviness of heart at the mention of Beth Garland's name. Here it was: the spotlight on local events. She turned the pages back.

A black and white photograph of Beth Garland's face confronted her. Without colour the vibrancy of the girl's hair was lost, but the face was definitely the same. *Beth Garland stars in city panto*, the headline said, and underneath, *Norchester's Royal Theatre has been fortunate in booking the West End pantomime* Sleeping Beauty *for a post-Christmas run of six weeks. Lovely songstress Beth Garland, whose meteoric rise to fame has been well documented in the musical press, plays the title role, with* . . . Trina scanned the lines, skipping details of the other actors until she came to *Married at 21, Miss Garland has swiftly taken the musical world by storm.* Trina bit her lip. She scanned the remaining lines. No further personal details, only a few words about Beth's other hit records.

She folded the newspaper back together and laid it aside. Married. So it was true. No mention of her husband's profession, or whether there were any children. Anyway, why should she care? They obviously adored each other—that had been clear in the way Giles Bayne had held Beth's hand last night.

'I've cooked you some bacon,' said Mandy as Trina sat down at the table. 'I hope you can eat it. Did you read the article?'

Trina nodded and reached for the teapot. 'Interesting.'

'Fancy her being married to a doctor,' Mandy said thoughtfully. 'Funny, isn't it—you don't expect the medical staff to be married to actresses somehow.'

'Is she an actress as well?' Trina's tone was casual. 'I thought she was purely a singer.'

'Well, they're versatile, aren't they?' Mandy pushed two pieces of bread into the toaster. 'You know show-biz people, they can turn their hands to anything in their line. By the way, did you see Alan's face when she was singing last night? He was absolutely riveted!'

'Was he?' Trina reached for the butter. 'I know he was pretty fed up at the beginning of the evening, poor chap. He feels everything's a bit pointless at the moment.'

'Why don't you two get engaged?' Mandy asked suddenly. "You're very fond of each other, aren't you? What's stopping you?'

Trina smiled. 'Plenty. For a start, we don't love each other.'

'Oh, I rather thought you did. You always give that impression.'

'Do we?' Trina was startled. 'I can't think why.'

'Look at you last night,' Mandy told her, 'just before

Beth Garland sang. Holding hands and gazing into each other's eyes—I can't see how you can say you don't love each other. Oh yes, I saw you! So did Dr What's-his-name, Beth's husband. He was concentrating all his attention on you at one point, only you were too besotted with Alan to notice.'

'Don't be ridiculous,' Trina said crossly.

'Did he *really* ask you out?' Mandy was curious. 'What actually happened? You were in such a state when you came in that I couldn't get any sense out of you.' She put a plate of bacon and eggs in front of each of them and sat down with relish to tackle hers. 'Come on, what did he actually say? I'm dying to know.'

Trina cut into her bacon. 'He asked me if I was doing anything this evening—at least, he meant last night. He asked if I was busy.'

Mandy raised her eyebrows. 'Did he, indeed! And you said?'

'I told him I didn't go out with married men.'

'And?'

Trina sighed. 'It was awful. He said he hadn't been asking me for a date, he was merely enquiring, as a matter of interest, if I had any plans for the evening.'

Mandy made a face. 'Sounds a bit odd to me. What else did he think you'd assume?' She took a mouthful of bacon and egg. 'No wonder you were cross! It must have been dreadfully embarrassing.'

'It was,' Trina said heavily. 'Look, do you mind if we change the subject? I've got to work with the wretched man and I'd rather forget him off duty, if you don't mind.'

'Sorry,' Mandy said cheerfully. 'Though I think you've sparked his interest, and I rather suspect it's mutual. What a pity he's married—they're always the worst. Sorry, change the subject. Don't forget you've promised to take Darren that Monster card, will you? Kids don't forget things like that, you know.'

'I won't forget,' Trina promised. 'I could take it into him this morning, couldn't I? It's a pity to keep him waiting until lunchtime. Sister Potts wouldn't mind, would she?'

'Of course she wouldn't—she thinks it's great for the kids to have visitors. Come on, eat up that lovely breakfast! Get a bit of food inside you and you'll soon cheer up. It'll keep you warm too—it's freezing outside.'

Trina tapped on the office door before she entered the Children's Ward. 'All right if I go in and see Darren?' she asked Sister Potts, who was sorting through patients' notes.

'Of course, dear,' The Ward Sister knew Trina. 'Stay as long as you like, the poor child gets terribly bored. Anything to keep him occupied!'

Darren's face was blank when Trina went in through the swing doors and approached his bed, which further depressed Trina's spirits. Darren didn't even recognise her.

'You're not going to give me an ninjection, are you?' he demanded suspiciously as she drew up a chair. 'I don't like ninjections.'

Trina chuckled. 'Of course I'm not. I've come to give you the Monster card. Don't you remember? I promised I'd give it to you if you ate up your Weetabix yesterday morning—remember?'

Darren peered at her. 'You haven't got your nurse hat on! You got ordinary clothes on. Where is it, then?'

Trina felt in her handbag and brought out the lurid card. She handed it to him.

'Cor, smashing!' he exclaimed, grabbing it. 'I ain't got this one, Cor, brill!'

Trina looked round the ward. Apart from the orthopaedic beds and a couple of sleeping children, there were hardly any of the usual small bodies charging about. 'Where is everyone?' she asked.

'In the playroom,' Darren informed her. 'A lady's come what's talking to 'em, telling them things and that.'

'Oh, I see. A teacher.'

'No!' said Darren with irritation, 'not a teacher. A special lady. She's showing 'em how to play cards.'

'Oh.' Trina paused. 'So when are you going home?'

'I dunno, do I,' the child said. He frowned, peering at her. 'Why have you got them earrings in?'

Trina fingered her neat gold sleepers, trying to disguise her amusement. 'Because I like wearing them. Don't you ever wear things you like?'

He gave her a scathing glance. 'Course I do. I got a space suit at home what I wear all the time, dun I?'

'Do you?'

'Course I do. My mum gave it to me for Christmas.'

'What about your dad? What did he give you?'

Darren looked blank. 'I ain't got a dad,' he announced.

Oh dear, Trina thought, I'd better be careful.

'I got a nan,' Darren said thoughtfully. 'She looks after me when my mum's at work.'

Sister Potts came into the ward and approached them. 'So you know this young man, do you, Staff?'

'Not really,' Trina smiled. 'But I promised him a

Monster card from our cereal packet yesterday morning, that's why I'm here.'

Sister Potts winked. 'Oh, I see. Have you seen what's going on in the playroom?' she asked. 'Great excitement! Go and have a peep.'

Intrigued, Trina tiptoed over to the playroom at the side of the ward. Behind the closed glass doors she saw a group of children clustering eagerly round a girl with long red hair. They were utterly absorbed, their eyes staring up at her adoringly. The girl turned her face to speak to a small boy, and Trina realised who she was at once. It was Beth Garland!

She tiptoed back to Darren's bed, where Sister Potts was pouring out a drink of blackcurrant juice. 'She's incredibly good with them,' said Sister Potts, handing Darren the drink. 'Come on, young man, drink this up—it'll help that leg to heal quickly. She's been here since half-past nine, telling them stories and playing cards with the older ones. Lovely girl. I just hope we can keep it quiet or the press will have a field day!' She took the empty glass from Darren's hand. 'Do stay for a bit longer,' she said aside to Trina. 'Darren's been feeling rather left out. I can't get his bed through the playroom door, or he'd have been able to join in. You haven't got to hurry away, have you?'

Trina looked at her watch. It was eleven-thirty. 'I'm on duty at one, I'll have to go soon after twelve.'

'Do stay till then if you can. The children have their lunch at twelve, so if you could entertain this young man here till then, you'd be doing us both a favour.'

'Of course I will,' said Trina. 'If Darren's got any games, we could play something together.'

Sister Potts looked thoughtful. 'There's some

Plasticine in the office, I'll get you that. Perhaps Staff Nurse will make you something with it,' she said brightly to Darren.

'Cor, yeah!' Darren said eagerly, his eyes gleaming. 'Monsters!'

Five squashed snakes and two dinosaurs later, the playroom door opened and Beth came out, followed by an eager crowd of small children. Some of them had patches over one eye, obviously post-operative squint repairs, Trina guessed, and an older girl in a dressing-gown who walked gingerly as if fearing for her abdominal stitches. Appendix, Trina smiled to herself.

She watched Beth Garland from the chair beside Darren's bed. The girl was wearing a long red corduroy skirt this morning and a sweater embroidered with coloured flowers. Seeing Trina beside Darren's bed, she came straight over to them. 'Hello!' she said cheerily to the child. 'What's your name?'

'Darren,' said Darren. He looked Beth up and down. 'What's your name?'

'I'm Beth,' the girl said. She turned to Trina with a smile. 'Are you Darren's mum?'

Trina shook her head. Close to, Beth was even lovelier than from afar. She was beautifully made up with a flawless skin, but there was something wistful about the dark shadows under her eyes and her mouth drooped slightly at the corners. 'No, I'm only visiting this old gentleman here.' She looked at her watch. 'I've got to go in a moment.'

'I'm not an old gentleman!' shrieked Darren indignantly, cackling with mirth. 'You're an old lady, ha ha!'

'Shh!' Trina eyes met Beth's with amusement. 'You're

Beth Garland, aren't you?' she asked politely. 'I heard you sing in the pub last night. You were fantastic.'

Beth drew up a nearby chair and sat down. Some warmly evocative perfume emanated from her. 'You don't mind if I join you for a moment, do you? Did you really enjoy it? Giles warned me I might be asked to sing.'

'It was marvellous,' Trina said warmly. 'The strange thing was that I heard your recording of that same song on the radio a little earlier. I thought it was fantastic then.'

'You're very kind,' said Beth, rather wistfully. 'It's a lovely song, isn't it? Gerry Parker wrote it for me and I recorded it about three weeks ago—it's only just been released.'

'Your name,' Trina said. 'You don't use your own surname?'

Beth shook her head. 'No. I took my stage name —Garland—from the wonderful, fabulous Judy. Of course I don't sing like she did, or even in her style, but I think Beth Garland sounds much better than Beth Bayne, don't you?' Her shoulders seemed to droop a little. 'I—I didn't want to use my married name. Tell me about you. Why are you visiting this lad here? Is he a relative?'

'No,' Trina confessed, 'I've only just popped in for a few minutes. I'm a staff nurse here at the hospital and I——'

Beth's face brightened. 'Then you must know Giles! Giles Bayne!' She frowned. 'Of course, you might not, he's only just started here at the General. *Dr* Bayne. Have you met him yet?'

Trina nodded. 'Yes. He's joined Mr Prosser's team,

hasn't he? I—I met him for the first time yesterday. He seems to have made quite an impact already,' she added carefully.

'Oh, that's Giles all right,' Beth laughed. She reached out and took a lump of Plasticine from Darren's fingers. 'Let me make you an elephant. I once got a star at school for one of these.' She rolled out four stumpy worms and squashed the ends flat for feet. 'Now, we'll need a piece for the body, one for the head and two for the ears . . .'

'I'll have to go,' said Trina, looking anxiously at her watch, 'I'm on duty at one.' She stood up. 'It's lovely to meet you, Miss Garland.'

'Call me Beth,' said the girl at once. 'And you're——?'

'Trina. Trina Morgan.'

'Trina,' said Beth, shaking hands. 'Perhaps we'll meet again.'

'I hope so.' Trina picked up her handbag from the back of the chair. 'Goodbye, Darren. Don't forget to eat your Weetabix at breakfast.'

'Course I won't!' Darren said scornfully. 'I *told* you, I like Weetabix, dun I?'

To Trina's dismay, she almost bumped into Mr Prosser as she left the ward. He was standing in the corridor surrounded by white-coated figures: his registrar, his secretary, Dr Rodney and others and Dr Bayne!

'Steady, Staff Nurse!' Mr Prosser said gravely as he steadied Trina's elbow with his hand. He gave her a suave smile. 'Been drinking again?'

'I'm sorry, sir,' Trina said ruefully, detaching herself, 'I didn't realise you were out here.' She made to escape, but Mr Prosser still had hold of her arm.

'This young lady is one of our home-grown staff nurses,' he said, dragging Trina forward and depositing her in front of Giles Bayne. His grey eyes looked down at her with amusement. 'She's one of our best, I'll have you know,' the consultant went on. 'Works on Merton Ward. Have you met Dr Bayne yet?' he asked her, and Trina nodded, blushing furiously.

'Shake hands, then,' Mr Prosser ordered with a smile, mortifying her even further. 'Go on, go on! He won't bite you!'

Not quite sure whether he was serious or not, Trina looked helplessly at Giles, who calmly held out his hand to her, a wry smile playing at the corners of his mouth.

Trina couldn't possibly get out of it. She shook hands awkwardly, wishing the floor would open and swallow her up.

'All right, lassie, you can go,' Mr Prosser relented at last, his eyes twinkling at Trina, and she fled gratefully.

'Nice little thing, isn't she?' she heard Mr Prosser remark casually to his entourage as she turned the corner, 'Damn good staff nurse. Neat little figure too.'

Trina dived into the safety of a nearby ward's linen cupboard, closed the door behind her, and stood there trembling with a mixture of amusement and exasperation. What a thing to happen! Why on earth did the surgeon's team have to be there at that precise moment? What a ridiculous thing to happen!

She stood there in the semi-darkness for a minute or two until she had regained her composure, then shook herself. Oh well, no great harm done. But as she hurried down the stairs and corridors towards the locker room glancing anxiously at her watch, she was uncomfortably aware of the fact that, married or not, the moment Giles

Bayne had taken her hand in his and their skin had made contact, she had experienced an ache of longing unlike anything she had ever known before—a quite ridiculous feeling of *rightness* and *belonging*. She was going to have to concentrate very very carefully in future in order to keep her feelings well under control!

CHAPTER FOUR

BY THE TIME she reached Merton Ward at one, Trina was well in command of herself again. Sister Price was off duty that afternoon and she gave Trina a brief Report before she went to lunch, going through the Kardex fairly quickly and pausing at Mr Spinks. 'He's fine, he's going home on Thursday, Mrs Knibb went home this morning—it probably was cholecystitis, but Mr Prosser's put her on the waiting list as her daughter's getting married next month—it'll be easier from her domestic point of view if she comes in later in the year . . . Mr Dalby. He's making good steady progress. One ounce of sterile water hourly by mouth and no more. He's to have the usual rotation of IV fluids, his drip's still in situ. I shouldn't think you'll have any problems this afternoon, Staff, we're fairly quiet.'

'Let's hope not,' Trina said, crossing her fingers mentally.

'Oh, and make sure Mr Dalby expands his lungs and does his physio exercises regularly, won't you, dear. The last thing the poor man wants is hypostatic pneumonia. He knows what to do—Physio were with him this morning.' Sister stood up. 'Oh, just one other thing. As we've got both the side-wards empty, there's a patient coming down to us from ITU.'

Sister Price reached for her handbag. 'They're very pushed up there, and I'm sure we can cope with him. He's a fairly young man, a head injury—unconscious but stable. They've had him up there like that for six weeks now, and they desperately need his bed. Mr Prosser has decided in view of the prognosis that there's not a lot of point transferring him to the neurological unit at Paxbury.'

'No?' Trina raised her eyebrows.

'No. They can't do anything for him there that we can't do here—two-hourly turns, oral toilet, etc. He's not on a respirator, he's breathing well on his own, and let's hope it will be just a matter of time before he regains consciousness.' She moved towards the door. 'Well, I'm off. Dr Bayne's on call if you need him.'

Trina made straight for Mr Dalby's bed when Sister Price had left the ward. He was sitting propped up wanly with an IVI in situ, looking a considerably better colour than the last time she had seen him.

'Hello, Nurse,' he said, smiling feebly as Trina approached. 'Still in the land of the living.'

'So I see,' Trina said approvingly. 'How are you feeling?'

'Great.' He pointed to his mouth. 'I could murder a pint of bitter.'

'Won't be long now,' Trina assured him. 'Meanwhile I'm afraid you can only have this stuff.' She held up the sterile water, then checked his fluid chart. 'You haven't had your one o'clock tot yet, I see.' She poured out an ounce of sterile water and handed it to him, then filled in the chart.

Mr Dalby sipped gratefully. 'Mr Prosser came round with that new doctor this morning. Says they've cut the nerve to the stomach, or something. What does that mean?'

'The vagus nerve,' Trina explained. She took the

empty medicine glass from his hand. 'They often do that with this kind of operation. It helps to keep the stomach calm.' She patted his hand. 'Don't worry, it's purely routine.'

'I know they know what they're doing,' Mr Dalby said gratefully. 'You medical people are wonderful. If it hadn't been for my operation I suppose I'd probably have died, wouldn't I?'

'Quite likely,' she agreed. 'They fixed you up in the nick of time. As long as you stick to the rules you'll be fine, but no pints of beer or steak and chips for a while, I'm afraid.'

She moved on round the beds, satisfying herself that all was in order.

At two o'clock the Introductory Block students came on to the ward again, Nurse Patel looking neat as a pin as usual and Nurse Stevens looking not quite so poised. Her cap was so far back on her head that it looked as if it was going to fall off at any moment.

Trina took her to the nurses' station, out of the patients' earshot. 'Put your cap further forward,' she told the girl. 'You won't be able to concentrate on a thing if you wear it like that.'

'I'm sorry, Staff.' Nurse Stevens readjusted it. 'Is that better?'

'Much better.' Trina regarded them both. Nurse Patel's brown eyes looked up at her steadily, and Trina frowned. Nurse Patel reminded her of someone—who was it? Mrs Patel! she thought suddenly. The name! I wonder if there's a connection.

She looked thoughtfully at the girl. 'You haven't got any relatives in Norchester, I suppose, have you?' she asked with interest. 'There's a family in the downstairs flat from mine with the same name as yours.'

Ira Patel smiled shyly. 'My aunt,' she said, nodding. 'She says she has three staff nurses living above her flat. I think she had promised you her recipe for *rogan josh*?'

'That's right!' smiled Trina. 'Her meals always smell absolutely delicious—I'm dying to try one out. What is *rogan josh* exactly?'

'It's a sort of lamb stew,' said Ira Patel. She felt in her pocket. 'I have the recipe here.' She handed Trina a piece of folded paper. 'My aunt is very shy about her English, so I wrote it out for her. I knew I would see you this afternoon.'

Trina pocketed the folded paper. 'Lovely, thanks. I'll get the ingredients when I go to the shops tomorrow. Now, to get back to this afternoon. I want you both to make up the bed in the first side-ward as an admission pack. We've got a patient coming down from ITU at about three—he's unconscious, so it'll be a good opportunity for you both to put some basic nursing into practice. Don't look so alarmed, he's stable. It won't be too bad.'

'Why is he unconscious?' Ira Patel wanted to know.

'A head injury, apparently. We'll have a look at his notes later and see what happened. Off you go and make up the bed. And Nurse Stevens—have you washed your hands recently? They look rather grubby to me.'

'I'm sorry, Staff!' Nurse Stevens looked stricken. 'I forgot!'

'Well, go and do it now. One thing you learn pretty quickly on a surgical ward is that you wash your hands on average three times an hour! Don't ever forget—the germs you take for granted in civilian life could kill someone if they got into a surgical wound.'

Trina showed them where the side-ward was and glanced about her. There was an oral toilet tray already made up on the locker with a set of post-anaesthetic instruments in a receiver, standard for nursing an unconscious patient. She fetched a ripple mattress from the linen cupboard, put it on to the bed, explaining to the students how it worked, then supervised them as they made up the bed-pack to receive the patient.

By the time she had finished the two o'clock medicine round, changed Mr Dalby's IV saline bottle for a litre of Dextrose/Saline and re-regulated the drops in the giving-set, the patient had arrived from ITU.

Leaving the auxiliaries to keep an eye on the main cubicles, Trina went to admit him. He was a young man of about twenty-four, thin and wiry and deeply unconscious.

Trina received the details of his care from the staff nurse who had accompanied him down from ITU, and settled him in to the bed. Ira Patel helped her to unfold the bedclothes and tuck them over him, then Trina showed them how to make up a Turning Chart and fill it in.

'How does he eat?' the Indian girl asked, watching Trina arrange his limbs so that there was a minimum of pressure on each. 'He is not on an intravenous infusion.'

'We feed him with fluid food.' Trina showed them the indwelling intra-gastric tube leading down the patient's nose into his stomach. 'Every two hours, with the mixture on this list here. We make it up in the ward kitchen, store it in the fridge, then give him so much of it every two hours down this tube.'

Both girls nodded. 'Looks like a lot of work,' Nurse Stevens observed glumly.

THAT HAUNTING MALADY

'It certainly is,' Trina said briskly. 'Now, I'll show you both how to make it up, then you can do it yourselves under supervision.' She took them into the kitchen and showed them the Complan, the vitamin drops bottle and the water to use.

Shortly after three-thirty, Giles Bayne appeared on the ward. 'I hear you've got the head injury from ITU, Sam Barlow. Where is he?'

'In the side ward.' Trina led the way, determined not to let her personal feelings show. They looked down together at the unconscious man.

'Mr Prosser's told me all about him,' said Giles. 'He's a builder, apparently fell off some scaffolding.' He consulted the patient's notes.

'Do you think there's any hope of him regaining consciousness?' asked Trina in a low voice.

Giles Bayne looked at her. 'Of course there is. There's every hope.' He bent over the unconscious man. 'You're going to wake up in the next day or two and talk to us, aren't you, Sam?' he said encouragingly to the patient.

There was no response, and Trina sighed. 'Poor man! We didn't get any reaction either. I think he——'

To her surprise, Giles took her firmly by the arm and marched her swiftly outside the room. In the corridor he turned and said to her with unexpected fury, 'Look, Staff Nurse, I don't care what the hell you think, but whether a patient is conscious or not, there's a growing body of evidence to suggest that he or she can still hear. Don't ever let me hear you speak in such negative terms in a patient's earshot again, conscious or unconscious —do you understand?'

'I'm sorry!' Trina gasped. 'I never thought. I——'

'Well, think in future!' he said coldly. 'I should have

thought a first-rate staff nurse like Mr Prosser seems to think you are would have known something as basic as that. Hearing is the last of the senses to go and the first to return. You just be damn careful in future.'

Trina blushed scarlet. 'There's no need to be quite so aggressive,' she said defensively. 'I won't make that mistake again.'

'There's every need,' Giles said angrily. 'How the hell do you expect patients to recover if you stand there suggesting negatives to them? You should know by now that these days we suspect the attitude of mind is paramount in a patient's recovery, even if he is unconscious. Infuse him with positive ideas, and you may just get results.'

His bleeper started to buzz. 'Don't forget in future,' he said grimly, then turned and walked towards the ward.

Trina followed him miserably. Why did she always get off on the wrong foot with him?

He entered Sister Price's office to answer the phone. 'Dr Bayne,' he said, picking up the receiver. 'Ah, good afternoon, sir.' He waved her away.

Trina went miserably. She collected the two new students and took them both to one of the female cubicles where Mrs. White, a jolly and helpful elderly lady who had had her appendix out the week before, was reclining on her bed, listening to the hospital radio service through earphones.

'Hello, Mrs White.' Trina introduced the new nurses. 'I wonder if you'd mind if we took your blood pressure.'

'Nothing wrong, is there, nurse?' Mrs White looked momentarily worried.

'Nothing wrong at all,' Trina smiled. 'You're doing

beautifully. But it would be useful if we could borrow your arm to practise taking blood pressure. That is, if you don't mind?'

'Not at all, dear!' Mrs White looked delighted. 'Help yourselves. I'm glad to be useful.'

Trina fetched the sphygmomanometer, applied the cuff to Mrs White's willing arm, and showed Nurse Patel how to pump up the cuff, then to listen through a stethoscope for the systolic beat as the air was let gradually out again. Nurse Patel learned quickly, then it was Nurse Stevens' turn. Trina soon had them fairly competent. She thanked Mrs White, removed the sphygmomanometer and put it back in its place on the table, promising Mrs White an extra biscuit with her afternoon tea for all her patience.

'That wasn't too bad, was it?' Trina asked the students. 'You both did very well. Congratulations.'

Then it was time for Visitors. They surged into the corridor, making for the various cubicles, clutching flowers, grapes and magazines.

Before they went into the side ward to turn Sam Barlow for four o'clock, Trina took the students into the treatment room and explained carefully to them that everything said in the unconscious man's presence was to be positive and encouraging. 'Hearing is the last sense to go, and the first to return,' she told them, echoing Giles Bayne's words. 'It's vitally important to be clear on that. Assume he can hear everything you say, that it's all registering in his brain. Do you both understand?'

They nodded. Then they all went in to turn Sam. He was lying in exactly the same position as they had left him.

Trina bent over him. 'Now, Mr Barlow,' she said

brightly, 'this is Nurse Patel and this is Nurse Stevens. We're just going to turn you over.'

They turned him carefully and made him comfortable.

'When you're awake in a day or two, you'll be able to tell us all about yourself, won't you,' Nurse Stevens said loudly into his ear. She looked up at Trina. 'Is that all right?'

'That's the ticket,' said Trina, nodding. She wished Giles Bayne could have been there to hear them!

The afternoon wore on, the usual ward routine added to by the two-hourly treatments in the side-ward. Trina soon had both students well involved and found Nurse Patel surprisingly capable. Before five p.m. both the juniors were well used to the routine of turning Sam, cleaning his mouth, applying his eye-drops and filling in the charts accurately, and Trina was well pleased with them both.

They went off duty at five, and Trina rather missed their help. There was no further sign of Giles Bayne. By the time the night nurses came on at eight she had almost forgotten the earlier contretemps with him, although she was aware that he wasn't far from her thoughts, and tried hard to ignore the longing that kept creeping back when she remembered the touch of his hand.

Trina reached the flat to hear the telephone ringing as she climbed the stairs. 'It's for you,' Sarah told her as she came in through their front door. 'Alan.'

Kicking off her shoes, Trina took the phone. 'Hello, Alan. How's things?'

'Hello, Trina.' Alan sounded cheerful. 'Look, I'm going to try and get tickets for the pantomime tomorrow evening. I don't know how difficult it'll be, but they might have a couple of cancellations. Like to come with me?'

'Tomorrow?' Trina thought quickly.

'Yes. Are you off?'

'I'd love to. Yes, I'm off at five.'

'Good. We'll go together. I don't know what sort of seats it will be, might be right at the back, but I'll do my best.' He paused. 'What did you think of Beth Garland last night?'

'I thought she was absolutely terrific,' Trina told him. 'By the way, I met her this morning.'

'Did you?' Alan sounded intensely interested. 'How?'

'She was on the Children's Ward. She's very good with children. She was telling them stories and playing cards with them all morning, apparently.'

'Was she?' He paused. 'What were *you* doing up there?'

'I went to see one of the kids,' Trina told him. 'An angelic little horror called Darren who's in traction, if that doesn't sound like a contradiction.'

There was a slight pause. 'Don't the staff mind if people go and visit the children? I thought you had to be a relative.'

'No, not at all,' chuckled Trina. 'Sister Potts—that's the Ward Sister—was glad of it. This boy gets pretty bored stuck there in traction all day. Why are you so interested?'

'Oh, no reason,' said Alan. 'Fancy you meeting Beth Garland up there. Did you speak to her?'

'Yes, she was amazingly friendly, just like anybody. Not at all unapproachable.'

'Tell me all about it when I see you,' Alan said. 'Do you feel like a drink tonight?'

She flexed her aching shoulders. 'No, not tonight, if you don't mind. I could do with an early night.'

'OK, I understand. Tomorrow, then. I'll pick you up at six. We could go for a meal first, if you like.'

'Lovely,' said Trina. 'See you.'

She had just put the receiver down when the phone rang again, and she picked up the receiver, assuming it was Alan with an afterthought. 'Hi there again,' she said warmly.

There was a slight pause. 'Is that Staff Nurse Trina Morgan?' It was Giles Bayne's voice.

Trina's heart began to thump. 'Yes,' she said, rather unsteadily. Giles Bayne phoning her at the flat? Whatever for?

'Look, I'm sorry to ring you at home,' he said, his voice sounding crisp and familiar, 'but it's about Sam Barlow.'

Trina's heart, which was already thumping, now gave a lurch. 'He's all right, isn't he?' she said anxiously.

'He's just the same,' Giles said. There was a slight pause. 'Look, I'm sorry I got so riled with you this afternoon. It's been worrying me. It was rather unfair of me to come down on you like that for something that was a perfectly innocent mistake, but this unconscious hearing thing is a bit of a pet theory of mine. I feel rather passionately about it.'

'Oh.' Trina didn't quite know what to say. 'Well, it's nice of you to apologise.' She hesitated. 'It really wasn't necessary, though. I *was* to blame.'

'Nice of you to say so.' She could hear the wry tone in his voice. 'The thing is, I'm a weekend off soon. If I don't see you on the ward tomorrow, I may not have the opportunity of apologising until next week. That's why I rang now. I hope you forgive me.'

'It's quite all right,' Trina said, rather stiffly, 'I—er—I agree with you, actually.'

'You do?'

'Yes, I do. I've often noticed people report that they've heard things while they were supposed to be unconscious. After operation, that sort of thing.'

'Interesting,' said Giles. 'We must talk about it some time. By the way, Beth tells me that she was talking to you on the Children's Ward this morning. I didn't realise Joan of Arc was the patron saint of children too.'

'I'm not,' Trina said defensively. 'I'd promised one of the children something out of a cereal packet, that's all. I was merely fulfilling my promise.'

'Don't you like children?'

'Of course I do. But I'm not in the habit of visiting them like Lady Muck as a social duty.' Oh dear! That sounded as if she were criticising his wife. 'I—I mean, Beth was doing a far better job than me,' she added hastily. 'The children adored her.'

'Yes, she's marvellous with kids,' he agreed, 'I'm pretty proud of her. What did you think of her singing in the pub last night?'

'I thought it was superb.' Trina had to be honest.

'You'll have to see the pantomime,' said Giles. 'I haven't seen it myself yet, and apparently it's quite something. How about coming with me tomorrow night? Beth's given me two complimentary tickets.'

Trina wasn't sure she'd heard properly. 'I—I beg your pardon?'

'Tomorrow night. I wondered if you'd like to come with me. Would you? You can be perfectly honest.'

Trina hesitated before answering. A multitude of

emotions swept over her: despair that she had accepted Alan's invitation, joy that Giles should ask her, confusion—even anger, that he should assume she would even consider accepting.

'If you're remembering our walk back from the shop last night,' said Giles, 'in spite of what you assumed, I wasn't asking you out then. This time I am.'

Trina hesitated, torn between longing and principle. Then she answered heavily, 'And as I told you on our walk back from the shop last night, I don't go out with married men.'

There was a pause on the other end of the line. 'Married men?'

'Yes,' she said wearily. 'You're married to Beth Garland, aren't you?'

Another pause. Was he taken aback to discover she knew about his marriage? Had he assumed she didn't know?

'I see,' he said at last. 'Well, that's very creditable of you, I'm sure.' There was even a catch of humour in his voice. 'However, I wouldn't have thought accompanying me to the Royal Theatre to see my—er—wife in a pantomime constituted too grave a breach of moral etiquette, would you? After all, Beth would be well aware of our presence. It was she who gave me the two complimentary tickets.'

'It would to me,' Trina said shortly. She bit her lip, anguished at having to refuse, and furious with herself for not wanting to.

'Are you still there?' he asked after a few seconds.

'I'm sorry,' she said. 'In any case, I've already been asked out tomorrow night. Alan rang me just now.'

'Alan? Ah, the good-looking gentleman with you in

the King Canute last night. I see. Well, never mind, it was only a suggestion. Forget I mentioned it.' He rang off.

Trina put the receiver down. She could have burst into tears. She looked down at her hands and realised they were shaking.

Mandy came bursting into the hall. 'Oh, I've had such a fabulous day!' she trilled, then seeing Trina standing there, she stopped short. 'Are you all right, lovey? You look upset.'

'I—I'm fine.' Trina squared her shoulders. 'Never mind me. Tell me about your day. Did you get the ring?'

Mandy held out her hand. An emerald twinkled against a plain gold setting.

'It's beautiful!' said Trina, hugging her friend. 'I'm so thrilled for you, Mandy.'

They went into the kitchen to show Sarah, who was browning a cauliflower cheese under the grill. She took it out and put it on the table. 'Show me. Oh, Mandy, it's lovely. Where's Keith?'

'Gone home to phone all his relations,' Mandy told her. 'His mother's over the moon! She's already planning what to wear. We've seen the vicar, too. Eight weeks' time, the first Saturday in April. Oh, I'm so happy I could burst!'

They sat down to the cauliflower cheese.

'By the way, Trina,' said Sarah as she dished it up, 'I hear you were chatting to Beth Garland on Kids' ward this morning. Apparently she thought you were rather nice.'

Trina flushed. 'How on earth did you hear about that?'

'Oh, I hear all sorts of interesting things during the

surgeons' coffee,' Sarah said with a grin. 'You'd be surprised what you can learn by keeping your ears open! Giles Bayne was telling Dr Rodney that Beth had said she'd met you. He seemed quite interested in Dr Rodney's opinion of you, actually.'

Trina was startled. 'Opinion of *me*?'

Sarah chuckled. 'Oh yes, you've made quite an impact there, my girl. With both of them, it seems. Dr Rodney told him you were an excellent staff nurse, and then Dr Bayne said——' She stopped. 'No, perhaps I'd better not tell you that bit.'

Trina found herself shaking again. 'Go on.'

Sarah had begun to look rather uncomfortable. 'Come on,' she said quickly, forking into her cauliflower cheese, 'Don't let this get cold.'

'Now, Sarah,' Mandy put in in exasperation, 'you can't just leave it like that. Look at poor Trina's face! Come on, let's have the truth.'

'Oh, all right,' Sarah said rather unwillingly. 'Well, after Dr Rodney said you were an excellent staff nurse, Dr Bayne was rather quiet. Then he said "However, I gather she's rather a supercilious little thing, isn't she? That was the impression she gave me." Sorry, Trina, but you did ask.'

Trina swallowed uncomfortably. A supercilious little thing? Was that the impression she gave? How awful!

'Anyway,' Sarah added lightly, obviously trying to make up for her revelation, 'whatever he may think of you personally, he was certainly impressed with your work. And apparently Beth thought you were extremely nice.'

* * *

By the time she got into bed that evening Trina's mortification had subsided into sheer anger. Thank goodness I made it clear that I wouldn't dream of going out with him! she thought furiously as she yanked her duvet up round her shoulders. A supercilious little thing, indeed! Insufferable man!

Why on earth had he phoned *her* of all people over the pantomime tickets? And not only that, he'd made it clear they were only complimentary ones! What was he playing at, for goodness' sake? Some game of tag with her emotions? Damn it all, he was a married man!

She thought of Alan with sudden affection. Dear old Alan, so straightforward and understanding. She was suddenly very glad indeed that he had phoned her first. Whatever would she have said if Giles had phoned first?

She closed her eyes determinedly and tried to sleep. She must get to sleep; she was on duty at eight the next morning. Only a couple more days and she had a weekend off, thank goodness. She could get away from that dreadful man, forget about the ward and Beth Garland and——Trina opened her eyes, then shut them again, waiting for the sleep that refused to arrive to claim her.

She turned over restlessly. Why couldn't she get to sleep? Why did the memory of her hand in Giles Bayne's keep returning to haunt her emotions? Damn it all, it was only a handshake, it wasn't even a kiss! Whatever would his kiss be like? She shook the thought away angrily. I will concentrate on my weekend off, she told herself firmly. I will *not* allow myself to think about him. How am I going to get home? The train. Yes, the train, like I usually do.

Two hours later she was still awake. She sat up and

looked at the clock on her bedside table. It was nearly one. Sighing, Trina got out of bed. It was no good, she would have to go and make herself a hot-water bottle or she would never get to sleep at this rate. Yes, that was it—she was cold. That was what was keeping her awake. It must be.

She slipped on her dressing-gown and tiptoed into the silent kitchen. While the kettle boiled for her bottle, she remembered the railway timetable in the kitchen drawer. She would look up the times of the trains to Nottingham, that would keep her mind off that wretched man. A stab of pain sliced at her with the memory of those words, *a supercilious little thing*. No, she thought, I will not think of him. I will concentrate on my weekend off.

Trina opened the drawer quietly and searched among scissors and string. Her hand found the railway timetable. She turned to the relevant page and ran her finger down the columns of trains to Nottingham. Good, there was a straight-through one from Norchester on Friday afternoon, arriving at Nottingham at five thirty. She found a pen and underlined it in red.

She was startled out of her concentration by the shrill sound of the phone ringing in the hall. She leapt to her feet, glancing at the clock on the wall. One-thirty! Whoever would ring the flat at that unearthly hour? It must be Theatre ringing for Sarah.

She grabbed the receiver off the phone, praying that its sound hadn't woken Mandy. 'Who is it?' she hissed crossly.

There was no answer. Trina tried again. 'Hello?'

Still no answer. Puzzled, she waited. She shrugged, and was about to hang up when she caught the unmistakable sound of sniffing from the other end of the line, and a girl's tearful voice. 'Staff Nurse Morgan? Is that you?'

'Yes?' Trina was puzzled. 'Who is that?'

'It's Nurse Gant.' Prue's tearful voice came down the receiver. 'Oh, Staff, I don't know what to do!' It was followed by the sound of crying.

'Put yourself together,' Trina said briskly. 'Now, what on earth's the matter this time?'

More sniffs.

'Come on,' ordered Trina. 'You'd better tell me. What is it?'

'I hope you weren't asleep,' Prue Gant sobbed. 'But I just had to call you. I didn't know what else to do.' She sounded distraught. 'Mr Dalby's in terrible pain. He couldn't sleep, you see, so I gave him a cup of tea . . .'

Trina's eyes closed. 'You *WHAT*?'

'I gave him a cup of tea and—oh, Staff Nurse, I think it's done him some sort of damage inside . . . !'

Trina thought quickly. Mr Dalby's operation had been done yesterday. He was only having an ounce of sterile water hourly. His Ryles tube was still in situ and——'Have you aspirated his Ryles tube?' she asked urgently. 'That's the very first thing you should have done.'

'I can't,' sobbed Prue. 'I think it's blocked—I can't get anything up it. I've tried to get hold of Night Sister, but she's all tied up with a multiple RTA in Casualty.'

'What about Dr Bayne? Have you called him?'

'I can't!' wailed Prue. 'Whatever will he say to me? Oh, Staff, I'm terrified! Please can you come to the ward? You'll know what to do. Please!'

'I'm on my way.' Trina slammed the phone down. She pulled on the nearest garment, which happened to be her uniform dress, grabbed her coat and slipped into her duty shoes.

The curtains were pulled round Mr Dalby's bed when she reached the ward, and Prue was behind them, vainly trying to aspirate his Ryles tube with the syringe. She was pulling so hard on the plunger that Trina had to take it away from her forcibly. Prue was in tears.

Mr Dalby was sweating with pain and his pulse was racing. He looked relieved when he saw Trina, but seemed unable to speak.

'It's all right, Mr Dalby,' Trina said soothingly, 'It was that cup of tea that did it. We'll soon have that up again. Go and ring for Dr Bayne!' she hissed at Prue.

The girl stared at her in alarm. 'I can't!' she said, anguished. 'He'll tell me off again!'

'Ring him!' Trina almost barked at her, but Prue just stood there shaking.

Trina went to the phone. 'Dr Bayne,' she said quickly to the switchboard. 'Please ask him to come straight to Merton Ward—it's urgent. I can't leave the patient.'

She put the receiver down and went back to Mr Dalby. Prue was still standing there sobbing. Mr Dalby was pointing to his mouth, looking greatly distressed.

Trina picked up the syringe and tried again to aspirate the Ryles tube, slowly and gently. The plunger refused to give, but a thin streak of blood appeared in the lumen of the tube. Oh God, she thought grimly.

Mr Dalby pointed desperately to his mouth. He seemed about to choke. 'Get a torch!' Trina ordered Prue. This time the girl obeyed.

'Open your mouth,' Trina told the patient, and he did so. The Ryles tube could be seen snaking about at the back of his throat, not nicely vertical as it should have been. Mr Dalby started to cough and gag.

'The tube's in the wrong place,' Trina told him. 'I'll have to take it out.'

Mr Dalby nodded. His eyes were watering and he was gagging again. Without hesitation, Trina detached the thin strip of zinc oxide strapping that anchored the tube to his nose and pulled gently. The tube came sliding out, visibly blocked at the stomach end.

Trina was laying it in a receiver when Giles Bayne came round the bed-curtains. His eyes widened when he saw Trina in her dishevelled state, then went straight to the patient. 'What's the problem?' he asked grimly.

'The Ryles tube was in his pharynx.' Trina showed him the tube. 'And there's 150 mls of fluid down in his stomach that shouldn't be there.'

Giles put a hand on Mr Dalby's forehead. The patient was now able to speak. 'I think it was that cup of tea, doctor. Don't think I'm quite ready for it yet.'

Giles's eyes blazed. 'Cup of tea?' Astonished, he looked from Mr Dalby to Trina.

'I'm afraid so,' said Trina. She turned to ask Prue to lay up a tray for passing another tube, but the girl had disappeared.

'I feel sick!' gasped Mr Dalby, and Trina shoved a vomit bowl into his hand. 'Stay with him?' she pleaded with Giles. 'I'll go and get a tray.'

She found Prue crying in the treatment room, sobbing into a tissue.

'Where's the tray for another Ryles tube?' Trina asked, exasperated. 'Surely you've laid one up?'

'I can't,' Prue sniffed. 'I'm too upset. I've got a terrible headache and I feel sick.'

Without a word, Trina collected what she needed, grabbed three different sizes of Ryles tubes in packs, and returned to the patient. He was clearly still in pain. 'Do you want to do it?' she asked Giles.

He shook his head. 'You go ahead.'

Trina went to wash her hands. Returning, she found that Giles had opened a pack and had the new Ryles tube all ready lubricated. Silently he handed her the tube and a swab, then stood aside.

Trina poured an ounce of sterile water into the medicine cup and put it in Mr Dalby's hand. He gazed up at her, full of trust.

'Swallow a sip of that,' Trina told him. 'But only when I say so. Ready?'

Mr Dalby nodded. 'Anything you say, nurse.'

Trina fed the tube gently into his nose, and paused when it reached the naso-pharynx. 'Swallow,' she ordered, and Mr Dalby swallowed. Trina moved it on another inch. 'Swallow again.' Mr Dalby complied. Three more swallows and the fresh Ryles tube was home.

Trina picked up the syringe and aspirated gently, withdrawing more than 150 mls of pale grey tea. Mr Dalby heaved a slow sigh of relief. So did Trina!

'That better?' she asked the patient gently. 'Have another sip of the water.'

Mr Dalby nodded. 'Pain's going,' he said thankfully.

Trina aspirated again. This time the aspirate she withdrew was clear water and—to her great relief—no further sign of fresh blood.

Mr Dalby lay back on his pillows, exhausted. At least he looked more comfortable. Trina glanced at Giles. He was feeling the patient's pulse. They heard the ward doors open softly behind them, and Miss Earl, the Night Superintendent, came round the curtains. She stood silently watching the proceedings.

Trina made sure Mr Dalby was comfortable, and filled in his fluid chart. The patient now looked a lot calmer, and his pulse rate had settled down considerably. He caught at her hand as she turned to go. 'Thank you, nurse—you're wonderful.'

'As long as you're all right,' Trina told him. 'That's the main thing.'

They pulled back the curtains and tiptoed out of the cubicle. Luckily the other men were sound asleep. Trina took the receiver with the soiled tube into the sluice, where she tipped it into the bin. There was no sign of Prue Gant.

She went back to the nurses' station where Giles and Miss Earl were talking together in low voices. They turned enquiringly as she approached.

Miss Earl looked grave. 'Well, Staff Nurse, I think I'd like an explanation.' She looked Trina up and down. 'I didn't realise you were on duty tonight. You weren't here earlier when I did a ward round.'

'I'm not,' Trina said wearily. 'I'm actually in bed. At least,' she added hastily, 'I'm supposed to be off duty. I—er—I was called to the ward by the telephone.'

'Where's Nurse Gant?' Miss Earl looked baffled. 'I thought she was in charge of Merton tonight. Where is she?'

'I'm afraid I've no idea,' Trina answered truthfully. Giles was staring at her strangely. She supposed she did look rather peculiar—no cap on, no belt, and hardly appropriately groomed for duty.

'Hmm.' Miss Earl's voice was noncommittal. 'I'll see

if I can find that young lady.' She left the ward, striding purposefully up the corridor towards the ward doors, leaving Trina alone with Giles.

'What precisely happened?' He looked her up and down with far from approving eyes. 'Am I to understand Mr Dalby was given a cup of *tea*?'

'I'm afraid so. He was in considerable discomfort and the Ryles tube was blocked, so it wasn't possible to aspirate it back without passing a new one, as you saw. I thought——'

'You thought it necessary to call me?'

'Yes, I did. There was a trace of fresh blood in the tube and the suture line in the stomach could have been damaged from the strain of all that fluid. I was really very worried.'

'I should damn well think so!' He looked furious. 'Whatever possessed you to give a two-day post-op partial gastrectomy a cup of tea? My God, the consequences could have been serious if the patient had started vomiting!'

Trina suddenly felt extremely weary. She could have explained, but she felt shaky, exhausted, and not at all like standing there defending Prue Gant yet again. 'It was a mistake,' she said wearily. 'Just a ghastly mistake.'

Miss Earl came back into the corridor. She turned into the cubicles before she came back to them, doing a quick ward round with her torch. 'All seems to be in order,' she said with relief. 'Although where Nurse Gant has got to, I've no idea. What are we going to do? I can't leave the ward unattended, and all the spare staff are tied up in Casualty.' She turned to Trina. 'Could you possibly stay on the ward for another half an hour while I sort something out?'

Trina nodded wearily. Under the circumstances she couldn't really do much else. She followed Miss Earl up the corridor as the SNO headed for the doors. 'Miss Earl,' she said quietly, 'even if you find Nurse Gant, to be honest I don't think she's fit to be on duty. She's not making very rational judgments, I'm afraid. She's——'

Miss Early nodded. 'I understand. You'd better get back to the ward. I'll find her, don't worry. I suppose she's got the DDA keys?'

'Yes,' said Trina. 'That's one of the things I'm worried about.'

'Borrow anything you need from the ward next door,' Miss Earl told her. 'I'll get someone else here as quick as I can.'

Trina went back to the nurses' station. Giles had disappeared. She glanced into Sister Price's office, but he wasn't there either. She went to peep at Mr Dalby. He was actually dozing, and Trina didn't disturb him.

Miss Earl came back within the hour with Helen Wills, a capable third-year student in Prue Gant's set. After a brief report, Miss Earl left the girl with an auxiliary and told Trina she could go. Trina went thankfully, with a last peep at Mr Dalby. He was asleep, and breathing evenly.

She retrieved her coat and made her way down towards the main entrance, then avoided the busy Casualty area from whence sounds of activity were coming, dodging into a passage and trying a side door. It was locked. Blow. She would have to go through Casualty after all.

The chaos seemed to have calmed down a bit. She caught a glimpse of the back of Giles Bayne's dark head and white coat as she slipped out of the main doors into the icy night. She was too weary even to feel angry at the injustice of his accusation.

Reaching the flat, she undressed and got back into bed. It was twenty past three. Thank goodness she was off at five the following evening and could have an early night. Her last thought before sleep overtook her was to wonder where Prue had got to with the DDA keys, and remembering that tomorrow night she had promised to go to Beth's pantomime with Alan.

CHAPTER FIVE

THERE WAS a message for Trina from the Admin Office when she went on duty the next morning. Would Staff Nurse Morgan please go and see Miss Bastin, the SNO on duty, at nine-thirty. It wasn't a question so much as a summons, and Trina went promptly at the time requested; hospital etiquette required punctuality.

Miss Bastin smiled as she knocked on the door and entered—obviously this wasn't going to be a haul over the coals, and for that Trina felt relieved. She had been slightly afraid of what the reaction to her dash to the ward last night might be, but Miss Bastin looked kindly at her and told her to draw up a chair.

Trina did so. Miss Bastin looked at her over the top of her rimless glasses. 'I expect you can guess what I want to see you about, can't you, Staff Nurse?'

'Well, yes,' Trina confessed. 'I imagine it's about what happened on Merton last night.'

'Just so.' The SNO looked sympathetic. 'I'd rather appreciate your help in clearing up the mystery of what actually happened.' She paused, eyeing Trina. 'Apparently Nurse Gant ran off to the nurses' locker room with the DDA keys from Merton Ward about two a.m. Miss Earl found her there in a state of near hysteria, not making a lot of sense. I wonder if you could tell me your side of the story?'

Trina told her about the phone call. It passed through her mind that she could be guilty of betraying Prue, but there really wasn't any alternative—what was paramount was the safety of the patients. 'And it was a potentially nasty situation,' she finished. 'It was probably lucky that Nurse Gant did telephone me. She was much too frightened of what she had done to think of calling Dr Bayne—or even to think straight.'

Miss Bastin listened carefully as Trina finished her account. Then she said, 'Staff Nurse, I'd like to ask you a question in confidence. What's your opinion of Nurse Gant as a nurse?'

Trina hesitated. This was difficult. She had anticipated this question, but rather hoped it wouldn't be asked. She had her private doubts as to whether Prue should be in a position of such responsibility, but was reluctant to say so out of loyalty.

Miss Bastin nodded sagely. 'You don't have to make any comment, of course, if you don't wish to. Your hesitation tells me quite a lot.'

'She's terribly meticulous,' Trina said carefully. 'Although I'm not sure that's always——'

Miss Bastin smiled. 'I understand.' She paused. 'Nurse Gant is attending the Staff Clinic this morning —we've insisted upon it. It's my private opinion that she will have to think very seriously about whether to continue her training. We simply can't have senior nurses rushing off hysterically in the middle of duty, let alone the damage she might have done the patient. Thank you, Staff Nurse. That's all.'

Trina stood up.

'Oh, one further thing,' Miss Bastin said. 'I gather that Dr Bayne assumed *you* were responsible for giving Mr—er—Mr Dalby that cup of tea. It's been made quite clear to him that you were not, and that your action in coming to the ward—if unorthodox—probably prevented any further damage being done. I would like to thank you for your help.' Her eyes twinkled. 'However, don't make a habit of it. Your off-duty is your own time. The ward is not your responsibility twenty-four hours a day, even though it may feel like that sometimes. Thank you, dear. You're an excellent member of staff and we're glad to have you.'

Trina left the office feeling relieved. Sister Price had the ward DDA keyes back safely—apparently Miss Earl had relieved Prue of them when she'd found the girl in the locker room, and Prue was going to the Staff Clinic this morning. No doubt Dr Fellows would recommend sick leave or—the possibility that Prue might be sacked crossed her mind, but she shrugged it off as being out of her hands. If that happened, it happened. There was no point in the hospital employing a nurse who was so unstable in a crisis. It was neither fair to the patients nor to the nurse herself.

She bumped into Giles in the corridor. His eyes lit up momentarily when he saw her, then he became professional. 'Good morning, Staff Nurse. I take it you've recovered from last night?'

Trina smiled wanly. 'Just about, thanks.'

'I've just seen Mr Dalby,' he informed her. 'He seems all right this morning, thank goodness. I understand you weren't responsible for giving him that disastrous cup of tea, and I'd like to apologise for assuming you were.' His grey eyes regarded her. 'Am I forgiven?'

'Of course,' Trina said lightly.

'Your action with the Ryles tube saved Mr Dalby from considerable distress. Even though a suture line has knitted well after thirty-six hours, any strain on it is highly undesirable, as you no doubt realise.' He paused. 'Are you sure I can't tempt you into changing your mind about the pantomime tonight? Beth's very good, you know.'

'I'm sorry,' Trina told him, 'but as I've already told you, I'm busy.'

His eyes held hers. There was something in them she couldn't quite fathom. 'I must get back to the ward,' she said unsteadily, 'I—er——'

'Yes? You were going to say?'

'I—I hope you enjoy the pantomime tonight. I'm sorry I can't come with you.'

'So am I.' He was very close, and Trina fought down a ridiculous longing to reach out her hand and run her fingers through the hair at the back of his neck. She dragged her eyes away from his. 'I—I must go. I'm on duty.'

'Then I must let you go,' he said gravely.

She had turned from him and had taken a couple of steps when he called to her again. 'Trina?'

She turned back. 'Yes?'

'Although I can't persuade you to change your mind about tonight, what about the weekend? Perhaps I could persuade you to come out with us for a drink on Saturday evening?'

Trina swallowed. 'Us?'

He nodded. 'Beth and I.'

What was he offering her? Some sort of chaperoned arrangement? Before she could answer, Giles spoke again. 'No, how stupid of me—of course, Beth will be working. Sunday lunchtime, then. I've got a weekend off. We could all have a drink together if you're off duty.'

'I'd like that,' said Trina, 'but unfortunately I can't. I'm off duty this weekend too. I'm going up to Nottingham to see my parents.'

'Nottingham?'

'Yes, they live there.'

'How very extraordinary,' said Giles. 'I'd vaguely thought of going up to Nottingham myself this weekend. There's a conference at the University. When are you going? Friday? Why don't you let me give you a lift?'

Trina fought for an excuse. 'That's very nice of you, but——'

'How were you going? By train?'

She nodded, her heart racing. The thought of being with him all the way to Nottingham gave her a wave of joy. Then she remembered Beth, and the wave broke. 'I don't think that would be very advisable, would it?' she said lamely. 'What about your wife?'

A smile played about his lips. 'Oh, Beth isn't coming with me. As I've just told you, she'll be tied up all the weekend with the pantomime—there's a matinee on the Saturday and the evening performances as well. It would just be you and me.'

'Then I couldn't possibly,' Trina said firmly.

He waved her objections aside. 'Of course you could. What on earth's stopping you? I—' he paused, his mouth twitching, 'I may be a married man, but my behaviour is exemplary, I assure you.'

Trina went back to the ward, fighting with her own mixed feelings. The thought of travelling all the way to Nottingham by car with Giles made her feel dizzy with excitement, but the knowledge that he was married gave her a terrible pang of guilt. But why should she feel guilty? It wasn't as if she was going out with him; he was only offering her a lift in the direction he was going anyway, by all accounts. Why shouldn't she accept?

She tried hard to put Giles out of her mind as she concentrated on her work. Mr Dalby was looking much better this morning and had progressed to two ounces of sterile water hourly.

Trina helped Pat Raynes to sit him out of bed on a chair after his blanket bath. They supported the arm into which his IV was running on a pillow, and encouraged him to move his legs. 'I should think that drip will come down in the next day or two if you carry on making progress at this rate,' Trina told him as she poured out his eleven o'clock tot of water. She lowered her voice. 'No harm done last night, I hope?'

'No, I'm fine this morning, thanks, nurse.' Mr Dalby hesitated. 'That poor night nurse—will she get the sack?'

'Well, she'll certainly be off duty for a week or two,' Trina told him. 'She's very overwrought at the moment, as you must have realised. Her mother's been very ill.'

Mr Dalby looked sympathetic. 'Poor kid! You girls are marvellous, the way you cope. It's no wonder things go wrong occasionally, the pressures on you.'

'It's nice of you to take it like that,' Trina said warmly. 'Oh well, no great harm done, although I wish it needn't have happened. You're sure you feel all right this morning?'

'I feel quite a bit better.' Mr Dalby winked. 'That cup of tea may not have done much for my innards, but it did a whole lot of good to my thirst!' He winked. 'I'm fine, don't you worry. As far as I'm concerned, it's all forgotten.'

Miss Hammond came on to the ward towards the end of the morning to do a blanket bath with Nurse Patel and Nurse Stevens. As Mrs White, their obliging guinea-pig over the students' practising taking blood pressures, had gone home that morning, Trina suggested they practised on Mr Neville, a cheerful elderly man who was nearly ready to go home. When approached, he said he would be only too pleased to serve in the cause of learning.

'But behave yourself,' Trina told him, mock-sternly. 'These are very young student nurses, and blanket-bathing is a serious business.'

'I'll be as good as gold,' Mr Neville said with a grin. 'They can even take me teeth out and clean them for me.'

'That's the ticket,' said Trina, chuckling. She left the students in Miss Hammond's hands and went into the side-ward with one of the auxiliaries to turn Sam Barlow. Giles's orders in the matter of positive encouragement had been passed to all the ward staff, and everyone concerned with nursing the unconscious patient had reacted with interest. They had all built up quite a conversational relationship with Sam.

Trina found herself feeling unusually tired as the morning wore on, finding herself longing for sleep after the strain of the night before. She did the twelve o'clock medicine round with even greater care than usual, handing out the scheduled diuretics and pills, and double-checking the treatment sheets.

Sister Price came on duty at one. After she had received the Report she peered at Trina. 'Are you all right, Staff Nurse? You look rather pale.'

'Yes, I think so, Sister.'

'Well, if you must turn up for night duty as well as

days,' Sister Price twinkled. 'Yes, I've heard all about it from Miss Bastin. You'll be relieved to hear that Nurse Gant has been ordered to take two weeks' sick leave pending a decision being made about her future.' She paused. 'I'm afraid there will have to be an Accident Report filed in case of repercussions, did Miss Bastin tell you? You'd better do your statement now, in the empty side-ward. Then I'm going to send you off duty. You look rather poorly.'

'I'm fine really, Sister. Just overtired.'

'I'll be the judge of that,' Sister Price said firmly. 'It's all right,' she added kindly, 'Miss Bastin herself suggested it. You write your statement, then go off at lunchtime instead of five. We've got an appendix coming in, but we can cope, don't worry. You go home and catch up on some sleep.'

Trina was grateful. She took the Accident Form and went into the empty side-ward next to Sam's. It was occasionally used for sick staff, or even the odd private patient who had to be kept isolated for some reason. Her statement didn't take long to write: she simply related the facts—she had been off duty and called to the ward at one-thirty a.m. by the nurse in charge. Told that the patient had been given a cup of tea in error, she had taken the appropriate action: informed the houseman and changed the non-functioning Ryles tube. Careful not to imply any blame, she finished it and signed it *T. Morgan, Staff Nurse*.

The canteen was busy with gossip at lunchtime. Everyone seemed to assume that Prue Grant had been sacked. Almost too tired to eat, Trina found herself having to defend Prue yet again. 'She hasn't been sacked,' she told everybody who asked her about the previous night, 'she's been sent off sick.'

'Trust you to defend her!' Pat Raynes said, over her salad. 'If you ask me, she ought to be given the push. She's utterly useless—more a liability than anything. If it was up to me, I'd sack her before she did any more damage. The girl's a neurotic mess!'

'Well, it isn't up to you,' Trina said shortly. 'Nor me. Thank goodness *we* don't have to make the decision. I think she'll probably be fine as soon as her mother's better. She's in an acute anxiety state at the moment, it's no wonder she can't think straight, poor girl. The fact is that we're *all* capable of cracking up if the pressures get too great, every one of us. Don't let's forget that.'

'Hmm, that may be so.' Pat looked unsympathetic. 'But the point is that you can't have patients put at risk. They may have sent her off sick temporarily, but I'll bet she'll get the sack in the end. You wait and see!'

Too weary to argue, Trina pushed her lunch aside and got up. She left the canteen, passing Sarah, who was sitting at another table with some of the theatre staff, tucking eagerly into sausages and chips. Sarah waved a hand absently, engrossed in conversation. Trina didn't stop to talk.

She went back to the flat, made herself a hot-water bottle, and got into bed in her underwear and dressing-gown, too tired even to undress properly. Pulling the duvet up round her shoulders, she fell asleep almost at once.

She awoke three hours later, feeling ravenously hungry and much refreshed. It was amazing what sleep could do. She had a bath and dressed leisurely, turning her radio into a local station to listen to the local news as she blow-dried her hair with Mandy's hair dryer. The announcer's voice was chatting easily, and Trina realised the guest was Beth Garland. She was only just in time to catch the tail-end of the interview, as Beth was being asked about her private life.

'Now of course, you're married, aren't you?' the interviewer was saying jovially. 'What about your husband? I suppose the lucky man's in show-biz too?'

Trina clicked the hair-dryer off, listening intently for Beth's reply. The girl hesitated for a moment, then she said, 'I—I'd rather not talk about that, if you don't mind.'

'Of course,' the interviewer said smoothly. 'Of course, that's fine. Well, it's been a great pleasure talking to you, Miss Garland. I know Norchester's delighted to have you here this season, and the pantomime's a smash hit. So, ladies and gentlemen, if you haven't already been, you'd better get on and grab those last seats, or you'll miss it. That's *Sleeping Beauty*, at the Royal Theatre—for another two weeks only. Now the news at five o'clock from our radio newsroom . . .'

Trina turned the radio off, wondering why Beth had been so guarded about protecting Giles. Perhaps, as he was a doctor, she had felt she should protect his professionality. She shrugged it off, determined to enjoy the evening, and turned her attention to deciding what to wear.

She was ready to go when Alan called for her at six. Now fully recovered from the previous night, Trina found herself looking forward eagerly to the pantomime. She had decided to wear a deep blue velvet skirt and white cotton lace blouse, as the Royal Theatre was sure to be warm in spite of the icy February weather outside. With deep blue studs in her ears, she did look rather nice, she decided on glancing into the mirror.

After a leisurely supper at an Indian restaurant near the Royal Theatre, they made their way through the icy streets together, Trina holding on to Alan's arm to avoid slipping on the frozen pavements in her high-heeled shoes. He had been unusually animated throughout their meal together, chatting easily about his work, which was unusual. He was wearing a dark grey lounge suit with a tie, his normally pale face alive with vitality.

They walked up the theatre steps together amidst a trail of adults in pairs and groups of excited children, and waited their turn in the foyer. Alan took their tickets out of his wallet and presented them to the usherette, buying a programme for Trina.

They filed into the auditorium and took their seats, Trina glancing about her with surprise: theirs were some of the most expensive in the house—in the middle of the third row from the front.

Before she could ask Alan how he had managed to get such good seats at such short notice, Trina had a further surprise—Giles Bayne was being shown into empty seats in the same row as theirs a few seats up from them, and behind him, dressed in blue lace and following him eagerly, was the portly but elegant figure of Mrs Prosser, the consultant surgeon's wife!

Trina looked away hastily, hoping that Giles hadn't seen her. The rows of seats filled up quickly, and soon she and Alan were well hidden by a large garrulous family who spent some time agreeing who should sit where, changing and rechanging seats and passing each other marshmallows.

Trina found herself feeling enormously excited as the orchestra filed into the pit and began to tune up their instruments. It was a thrill to come to the theatre, but even more so to know that she had met Beth Garland and could almost be said to know her personally. The safety curtain rose into the air, the house lights dimmed, and the orchestra began the overture.

Trina sank back into her seat, forgetting everything, spellbound, as the curtains opened. Half wondering whether Alan would reach for her hand, she was briefly surprised when he didn't. She smiled to herself, imagining Giles reaching for Mrs Prosser's hand, then forgot even Giles in the magic of the performance.

The pantomime was everything Trina had hoped it would be, and more. The scenery was wonderful, the dances full of colour and life, the peasants hilarious, the Dame so amusing that her sides ached from laughing, and the evil witch who had cast the spell upon the Sleeping Beauty hideous and just short of terrifying —but most breathtaking of all was Beth as the Princess Rosebud. Her long auburn curly hair shone with intense light, her voice was full and strong, and her wistful beauty seemed even more radiant under the powerful stage lights.

Casting a sideways glance at Alan during the third scene, Trina realised he was utterly lost. He was gazing up at Beth with sheer adoration in his face. And when Beth sang *That Haunting Malady*, which had been cleverly worked into the score, even Trina found her eyes filling with tears.

All too soon it was over. The grand finale swept to a close, the hideous witch was vanquished, the Princess was kissed awake and promised to marry the Prince, and the whole company took their bows and encores. Trina's hands ached from clapping. She clapped and clapped, wishing it would start all over again, wishing that the curtain never had to fall on the colour and music, that she could sit through it all over again. But alas and alack, as all pantomimes must, it all came to an end and soon the final curtain had fallen and they were all trooping out.

'Wasn't it lovely?' Trina's eyes shone. She turned to Alan. 'And Beth—wasn't she wonderful?' She glanced towards Giles filing out ahead of them, politely escorting Mrs Prosser, then back to Alan again. 'What did you think? Oh, Alan, thank you so much for bringing me! Wasn't it marvellous?'

'Superb.' Alan seemed quietly contained, and Trina wondered more than once at the look of suppressed joy in his eyes. 'You're very quiet,' she told him, mystified.

Alan's eyes were dancing. 'Ah yes,' he said, nodding sagely, but he didn't explain further.

Inevitably, they filed out behind Giles and Mrs Prosser as the queue of sleepy children and animated adults reached the foyer. Before Trina could dodge to avoid the dark head and broad shoulders ahead of them, Giles turned and saw her. His face seemed to tighten, then relaxed again into the familiar politeness she had come to expect from him. 'Good evening!' he greeted them, steering Mrs Prosser's elbow round to introduce Trina. 'Mrs Prosser, may I introduce you to one of our staff nurses? This is Trina Morgan and—er?'

'Alan Taylor,' Trina introduced Alan, as they all shook hands. 'What a wonderful pantomime, wasn't it?'

'Absolutely delightful!' Mrs Prosser enthused. She

turned to Giles. 'And you must be very proud of Beth, Dr Bayne.'

'Oh, I am,' Giles said warmly. His eyes met Trina's. She looked away quickly, not daring to meet the challenge in them. 'I could hardly believe she belonged to me up there on the stage,' he went on, his words giving Trina a stab of longing mixed with despair. 'Magnificent, wasn't she?'

Mrs Prosser looked mildly surprised. 'But surely you must have seen her perform before?' she asked with raised eyebrows.

'To be honest, no, I haven't. It was quite an eye-opener.' Giles sounded amused. 'I've seen her on television, of course, but never live on stage before.'

'Well, you do surprise me,' said Mrs Prosser. She turned to Alan. 'Have you met Beth, Mr—er—Mr Taylor?'

To Trina's surprise Alan nodded. 'Yes, I have. And we both heard her sing a couple of nights ago, didn't we, Trina?'

Mrs Prosser's eyes fell on Trina. 'Well, it's nice to meet you both, my dear. Did I understand that you were engaged?' she asked with interest.

'Not yet.' Alan smiled. 'That is, I'd be honoured to be if we were, but we're not.'

Mrs Prosser nodded. 'Ah, just friends. That's nice.'

'I think we'd better go and find my car,' Giles was saying, as he guided Mrs Prosser carefully down the steps and out into the chill February night. 'Good night!' he called back over his shoulder to Trina. Then they were gone.

Trina and Alan made their way across the road to the car park where Alan's Renault was parked. As she got into the passenger side, she saw Giles escorting Mrs Prosser towards his BMW, opening the door for her and settling her inside.

'It's ten-thirty.' Alan looked at his watch in the light of a street lamp as he got into the driving seat beside Trina. 'We've got time to catch the Can if you like. Do you feel like a drink to round off the evening? I've got something rather interesting to tell you.'

'Yes, I'd like that,' said Trina, unwilling to let the evening end. So she hadn't been wrong about Alan; there *was* something on his mind. Her ears were still full of the music of the pantomime, and she felt she couldn't bear to go back to the flat just yet.

They drove out of the car park behind Giles's car, Giles turning one way to take Mrs Prosser home, and the Renault taking a left turn back towards the hospital.

In the warmth of the pub, they found their usual seats. The male nurses weren't playing this evening and the lounge was unusually quiet. Alan bought them a drink each, then sat there sipping his, seemingly lost in thought.

'You can't stop thinking of her, can you?' Trina said gently.

'Does it show so much?'

She nodded. 'Quite a lot, I'm afraid. Oh, Alan!'

'Wasn't she wonderful?' Alan's face glowed. 'When she came on in the first scene, I thought I was going to burst. I felt like standing up and cheering, and——' He caught at her hand suddenly. 'Oh, Trina, you don't mind, do you? I can't pretend—I've fallen head over heels in love with her. It's hopeless trying to deny it.'

'Of course I don't mind.' Trina patted his hand. 'We

had that sort of agreement anyway, didn't we? But Alan——'

'We can still go on being friends, can't we? I value your friendship tremendously, Trina. I'd like to think I'll always be able to keep it, whatever happens.'

'Of course—we'll always be good friends,' Trina assured him. But Alan——' She hesitated. 'Look, I don't want to preach, but aren't you rather letting yourself get carried away by a fantasy? Beth is a beautiful girl, I know, but she's——'

'You think I'm infatuated, don't you?'

Trina nodded. 'I'm rather afraid you are. She's famous, Alan. She's beautiful and talented, but you know absolutely nothing about her as a person. Besides which——'

'You're wrong,' said Alan. 'You're wrong. It's not just infatuation. I knew the very moment I first set eyes on her, even before I knew she was Beth Garland, that she was the only girl in the world I could ever fall in love with. I don't care what her past has been, I don't——'

'But—but she's *married*!' Trina said helplessly. 'It's absolutely insane to let yourself fall in love with a married woman. Oh, Alan, you must need your head examined! Whoever in their right mind would——'

'Married?' he said. There was a curious gleam in his eye. 'Well now, that's where you're wrong. She *was* married, I know. But her husband has left her. Eight and a half weeks ago, to be precise. And he's not coming back. They're in the process of divorce proceedings right now!' He grinned at her. 'So you see, I do have a chance, after all!'

CHAPTER SIX

TRINA stared at him, absolutely staggered. 'What?' she managed to gasp.

'They're separated,' Alan said calmly. 'Don't look so shocked. I'm not surprised you didn't know, it's not generally known. Beth doesn't like people knowing, but it's perfectly true.'

'But—but her husband!' Trina said shakily. 'Her husband's here at the hospital! Dr Bayne!' She shook herself. It didn't make sense. Giles and Beth didn't behave as if they were separated; there was obvious affection between them.

Alan grinned. 'Don't look so anguished, it's all right. Your Dr Bayne isn't Beth's husband—he's her brother.'

'Her *brother*?' Trina felt as if someone had hit her on the head with a mallet. 'But—but he said he was married!'

'To Beth?'

'Yes. No. Yes, I think so. At least, he certainly gave me the impression he was married,' Trina said faintly.

He shrugged. 'Well, he certainly isn't married to Beth. I suppose it's just possible that he lets it be thought that he is, to protect her. They're very close, those two.'

She was still trying to recover from the shock. 'How can you be so sure?' she asked, dazed.

Alan's eyes were dancing. 'Beth told me herself. That's what I wanted to tell you. How else do you think I got hold of those tickets?' He grinned. 'Where there's a will, there's a way.'

Trina stared at him, nonplussed. 'How do you mean? You've actually *met* Beth? *Talked* to her?'

He nodded. 'Remember you told me about meeting her on the Children's Ward the other morning? Well, I did a bit of conniving on my own. I was so desperate to meet her that I'd have done anything! So I went up there to visit this Darren of yours myself.'

'*You* did?'

He laughed. 'Why not? The kid loves visitors. I bought a toy car, and asked the Ward Sister—what's her name, the one with grey hair?—if I could go and talk to Darren and she said by all means. It was easy. Beth was there with the children again, and we got talking. For quite some time, actually.'

Trina took a sip of her wine, wishing it was brandy. She could have done with it for shock.

Alan smiled. 'Don't look so disapproving! Faint heart never won fair lady. Besides, I didn't do anything underhand—I just made sure I was in the right place at the right time.'

Trina was still trying to work it out. 'What happened?' she asked, dazed.

'I was chatting to the boy when Beth came over and said hello. Asked if I was his father. I said no, I'd just come to visit him, that a good friend of mine, Staff Nurse Trina Morgan, had told me the boy liked visitors. I enjoy kids anyway, you know I do, so it wasn't too far from the truth.' He paused. 'She sat down with us and we got talking. I asked her outright if she was married—that's when she told me about her separation. They're going to get a divorce. Apparently he ran off with a dancer, and there's no question of reconciliation. No children, you see. Apparently he didn't want them anyway. She said she was glad to be here in Norchester because it means she can see a lot of her brother who's just started work here.' He grinned at Trina. 'Simple, really. She seemed glad to talk. I don't think she meets many people, with the sort of high-pressure working life she leads.'

Trina had to admire his initiative. 'Well!' she said, rather at a loss. This was a side of Alan she'd never seen before. 'What can I say, other than good luck? Are you going to see her again?'

He winked. 'What do you think? Didn't you wonder how I got those tickets at such short notice when the box office had completely sold out? They were some of Beth's complimentary ones. She seemed quite glad to find someone who'd like to use them.'

Trina was still trying to recover her wits. She shook herself, trying to sort out her thoughts. 'But—but why did Giles—Dr Bayne tell me he was married?' she asked puzzled. 'I don't understand it.'

Alan shrugged. 'Does it matter?'

'Not at all,' she said hastily. 'But it's odd, that's all.'

'Perhaps he *is* married,' he suggested reasonably, 'to somebody else. Or as I said, perhaps he lets people assume Beth is his wife to protect her. Who cares?' He drained his glass. 'All that matters to me is that she's free—or will be, in a matter of months. Want another drink?'

'No, thanks.' Trina stood up. 'I think I'd like to go home, if you wouldn't mind.'

'OK.'

They walked back to the car, both of them silent with their own thoughts as Alan drove the short distance back to the flat and pulled up outside.

'Do you feel like coming in for coffee?' Trina asked him as she put her hand on the handle to open the door.

'No,' he said, 'I won't, if you don't mind.' He caught at her hand. 'Trina, you're very quiet. You're not hurt, are you, that I've fallen for someone else?'

'Of course I'm not.' She patted his hand reassuringly. 'I'm very glad for you, Alan. I hope desperately that it all works out.'

He seemed genuinely concerned. 'So we can still be friends?'

'Of course we can. And to prove it, how about coming round on Monday evening? I'll cook you a meal. Mrs Patel in the flat downstairs has given me a wonderful recipe for something called *rogan josh*—I'm dying to try it out.'

His eyes lit up. 'I'd love to. But why not tomorrow night?'

Trina shook her head. 'I've got the weekend off. I'm going home to Nottingham to see the old folks.'

'Are you? By train?'

'No, someone's giving me a lift.' For some reason she felt reluctant to tell him it was Giles—apart from anything else Alan might ask her to pump Giles for information about Beth. 'One of the staff is going to a medical conference at the University, he's offered me a lift. I'll be back late Sunday. Make it Monday evening, if that's all right with you?'

'Fine,' Alan agreed. He bent over and kissed her on the cheek. 'Good night, Trina. Thanks for coming with me tonight. It was great, wasn't it?'

'Wonderful,' she echoed. She got out of the car, pausing to lean in through the window. 'I wish you all the luck in the world, Alan. I mean that.'

'Thanks.' He smiled. 'Have a good weekend off. I'll look forward to Monday.' He drove off, waving.

There was a scribbled message for Trina when she reached the warmth of the flat. *Giles Bayne rang*, Mandy's firm writing informed her, *Will pick you up two p.m. outside flat*.

Trina sighed. She should have been excited at the prospect, but somehow she felt depressed. Why on earth hadn't she insisted on going by train? A whole hour in Giles's company all the way to Nottingham would be hopelessly embarrassing, given the way she felt about him now—unsure of her ground. Was he married or not? She shook herself crossly. What did it matter anyway?

She undressed and got into bed, waiting until she was curled up under the duvet before she allowed the flood of new thoughts to wash over her. Giles was not married to Beth. That changed everything—or did it? Perhaps he was married to someone else. Anyway, what if he wasn't? Why had she let her go on believing he was married? He hadn't contradicted her when she'd challenged him with it, had he—he had smiled in that wry way of his and let her go along with her assumptions. Why? Was he playing some sort of game with her?

What difference did it make to her, anyway? Furious with herself, she punched her pillow crossly. She was behaving like a love-struck schoolgirl. Damn Giles Bayne! It was ridiculous that he should fill her thoughts so much, especially as it was plain what he thought of her. Well, all right, not to her directly, but that was obviously his opinion of her—*a supercilious little thing*, indeed! Right, Dr Bayne, she thought grimly just before she fell asleep, you can give me a lift to Nottingham, but as for cosy little Sunday lunchtime dates with you and Beth—no, thanks! The last thing in the world I would want to inflict upon you is my supercilious company!

Trina still felt oddly cross and depressed at breakfast the next morning. She had slept fitfully, partly due to having had a sleep during the previous afternoon, and partly because her dreams had been full of Beth and Alan, with Giles ever-present behind them, watching her with that grey gaze she found so disturbing.

'Cheer up!' said Mandy, feeding bread into the toaster, 'I don't know what you're looking so gloomy about—a fabulous evening last night and a weekend off in front of you—you've only got to work till one. It's me who should be down in the dumps, I've got to work tonight!'

'Sorry,' Trina said ruefully. 'Bad night, that's all. I don't mean to be a pain. By the way, where's Sarah?'

'On call. I wonder if they were busy in the night.' Mandy peered into the toaster. 'Hurry up, I'm hungry!'

'You always are,' Trina told her with a laugh. 'It's just as well Keith doesn't like skinny women.'

'I'll never be that,' said Mandy with a sigh. She felt her hips anxiously. 'Do you think I ought to try and lose weight before the wedding? I'm going to look ridiculous walking up the aisle in a size sixteen, and if I carry on eating at this rate I will be.'

'You could lose a few pounds,' said Trina, looking at her, 'but I don't suppose it matters. Keith loves you as you are, I've heard him say so. Not every man likes a beanpole.'

'No, thank goodness,' Mandy agreed heartily. 'You've never had to diet, have you, lucky thing. You've always had a super figure.'

'The Morgan constitution, no doubt,' Trina told her. 'My father's as skinny as a rake, and I suppose I take after him.'

'What are your parents like, Trina?' Mandy looked wistful. Her father had died when she was small, and her mother only the year before. 'You're lucky to have both of yours.'

'They're lovely,' Trina said warmly, 'but very ordinary. My father's retired, rather quiet and reserved. My mother's just an ordinary nice person.'

'I wish mine had known Keith,' sighed Mandy.

Sarah came in at seven-thirty, just as they were finishing their breakfast. 'Thank goodness that's over,' she said, yawning. 'Nothing happened at all until four-thirty, then some wretched woman from Maternity decided to go into labour with a placenta praevia at crack of dawn, and we had a Caesar.'

Mandy winked at Trina. They both knew this was just talk: Sarah adored her job and wouldn't have changed it for the world.

'Is that toast I smell?' Sarah looked round for a towel, after washing her hands at the sink. 'Put a couple of slices in for me, Mandy.'

'Was the baby all right?' asked Trina.

'Oh, fine.' Sarah sat down at the table. 'A little boy. The obstetrician was tied up on the ward with another difficult delivery, so they got Mr Prosser in to do the section with Giles Bayne assisting. By the way,' she confided, reaching for the butter, 'a bit of gossip for your willing ears—I've heard on the grapevine that when

Beth Garland stayed in the Residency flats the other night, she and dear Dr Bayne had different rooms! Strange, isn't it?'

'Of course it's not strange,' Trina said crossly. 'Beth Garland isn't his wife or even his girlfriend—she's his sister.'

It was Sarah's turn to look startled. 'His *sister*?'

Mandy stared at her. 'How do you know?' she asked, intrigued.

'Because Alan got chatting to her on Children's Ward yesterday,' Trina told them. 'Apparently Beth's separated. Her husband ran off with a dancer.'

Mandy whistled. 'Well, well! Poor girl.' She looked thoughtful. 'So the dashing Dr Bayne isn't married after all . . .'

'I've no idea,' Trina said shortly. She felt her cheeks grow red as they both stared at her. 'He might be, for all I know. I'm really not bothered.'

'A little too vehemently said, don't you think?' Sarah said to Mandy with a knowing wink. 'Well, duckie, I don't blame you, you're not the only one to have fallen under his spell,' she added to Trina. 'Every unattached female in the hospital has fallen hopelessly in love with him.'

'Well, I haven't!' Trina said crossly. 'I don't even *like* the wretched man!'

'Oho, and he's taking you up to Nottingham in his car!' teased Mandy. 'You'd better look out, dearie—you're up against some stiff competition.'

'Look,' said Trina. 'He's taking me up to Nottingham because he happens to be going up there to a medical conference, and I happened to say I was going there to see my parents, that's all.'

Mandy and Sarah exchanged looks. 'Highly suspicious, I'd say, wouldn't you?' Mandy confided to Sarah. 'Especially now we know he's not married.'

'We don't know he's not married,' Trina retorted. 'We just know he's not married to Beth Garland, that's all. Look, I don't know why we're having this stupid conversation anyway. I can't stand the man, if you want to know the truth. I only agreed to accept a lift from him because I couldn't very well get out of it without being downright rude.'

'But you must admit he's attractive,' Sarah teased. 'Oh, those deep grey eyes, those broad shoulders, those capable hands!' She gave Mandy a quick wink across Trina's bent head. 'Not to mention the way he talks about you behind your back!'

Trina stiffened. 'What do you mean, talks about me?' Her shoulders sagged. 'Oh, I see, you mean the *superciliouslittle thing* remark, I suppose.' That still hurt.

'That and more,' Sarah laughed. 'You came up more than once in the conversation over the Caesar this morning. Mr Prosser was telling Giles how much his wife had enjoyed the pantomime last night—who were the charming couple Giles had introduced his wife to? he wanted to know. Giles said it was a certain Staff Nurse Morgan and her boyfriend, and Mr Prosser beamed and said, 'Ah, my little *bella bambina* from Merton Ward!' or something like that—you know how he's always going on in Italian—and Giles went rather quiet and said he didn't see you quite like that, more as a sort of poison! Then they both laughed and agreed.' She glanced quickly at Trina. 'Don't take it too much to heart, love—I'm sure Giles was only joking.'

Trina flinched. Poison! A sort of poison? The casual remark was cruel, and the thought that Mr Prosser had found it amusing hurt even more. She felt herself go hot and cold all over.

Mandy was asking her something. 'Did you find my note?' She patted Trina's arm. 'Cheer up, you'll only have to put up with him on the journey home, then you can forget about him for the entire weekend. I know! You can spend the time planning what you're going to wear as my bridesmaid! You will both be my bridesmaids, won't you? I want you in yellow, I think. Or perhaps a nice apple green. Oh, it's going to be fabulous, isn't it!'

By the time two o'clock arrived, Trina was ready. She had packed a bag containing her overnight things and a couple of jumpers she could wear with her jeans at home, and pulled on leg-warmers and her duffel coat. The atmosphere in the car might be frosty, but at least *she* would be nice and warm!

She stared into the wall mirror as she waited in the little hall. Did she look supercilious? Was she really poisonous? It was a horrible word. Hurt and angry, her eyes stared back at her. She certainly wasn't going to put herself out to be friendly after that!

By the time Giles's BMW arrived outside the flat, Trina's hurt had cooled to an icy fury. It crossed her mind that in giving her a lift all the way to Nottingham Giles was doing her a favour but, knowing that he was going that way anyway, she decided it wouldn't put him out much to drop her on his way to the University. Poison indeed! She'd show him!

The car drew up beside the kerb. Before Giles could

get out, Trina had closed the door of the flat behind her and reached the passenger door.

'Hello there!' he said cheerily through the open window. 'All ready?' He looked ridiculously attractive in mufti, his familiar white coat exchanged for a warm jacket with a dark wool rollnecked sweater underneath, and well cut slacks. 'Climb in. I'm glad you're on time. Good girl!'

Trina got into the passenger seat with her bag, annoyed with her heart for beating so furiously. 'Good afternoon,' she said coolly. 'I hope this isn't going to put you out too much.'

He took the bag from her hands and tossed it into the back. 'Of course it isn't. I told you, I was going that way anyway.' His glance flickered over her as he started the engine. 'You look nice and warm. I like the legwarmers.'

She tried to relax as he drove off through the familiar streets, but it was surprisingly difficult. What on earth were they going to talk about all the way to Nottingham? 'I hear you had a Caesarian at crack of dawn,' she said with a brave attempt at bright conversation. 'Sarah told me the patient was a placenta praevia.'

He looked puzzled. 'Sarah?'

'Staff Nurse Wade. In Theatre.'

'Oh, that's Sarah, is it?' He seemed amused. 'Did you enjoy the pantomime last night?'

'Very much,' Trina said. 'Your wife was wonderful.'

'My wife?'

'Beth, of course.'

He grinned to himself, but didn't reply. Hateful man, now she knew the truth. Was he carrying on the charade to torment her? Or did he have some other reason?

'What did you think of the evil witch?' he asked. 'I thought she was particularly good.'

'Excellent,' Trina said shortly, then lapsed into silence, looking out of the window. That lasted until they reached the turning that would take them out of the city and north towards Nottingham.

'You seem rather quiet today.' Giles's voice was light as he took the corner and changed up a gear. 'Have I said something wrong?'

'Of course not.' Trina tried hard to disguise her fury. Why wasn't she brave enough to be honest? Only pretended you were married, she wished she could say. And that I'm poisonous, and a supercilious little thing. She clenched her fists inside her gloves. 'I—I'm rather tired, that's all.'

He turned the radio on, and a lilt of Country and Western music filled the car. Trina began to relax a little. Perhaps it was childish of her to behave so rudely, but his proximity made it difficult to think straight. She tried hard to think of something civil to say. 'How did the Caesar go? A little boy, wasn't it?'

He nodded. 'It went well, thanks. The baby was fine—a nice little chap. Of course, the good thing about a section is that the baby suffers almost no trauma at all, other than the fact of suddenly finding itself hauled out into the world by a hand instead of having to go through the normal process of birth.' He glanced at her. 'You haven't done your midwifery training, I take it?'

'No,' said Trina. 'We had some obstetrics experience as part of our general syllabus, but I've never thought seriously about doing Midwifery. Not yet, anyway.'

'Have you been qualified long?'

'Just a year,' she told him. 'I got the post on Merton

immediately after my finals. I was lucky.'

'You're good, too.' His voice was warm. 'The way you handled that situation with Mr Dalby the other night was first-rate. Congratulations. Mr Dalby thinks you're wonderful.'

Trina flushed. Praise from Giles was unexpectedly warming. The Country and Western music changed to a smoochy ballad, the car was warm and comfortable, and she began to feel much more at ease.

'Tell me about yourself,' invited Giles as the winter landscape slid by. 'Have your parents always lived in Nottingham?'

'I grew up there,' she told him. 'My father was born there, but my mother is Welsh.'

'Aha!' he said. 'Your colouring—I should have guessed. Have you any brothers and sisters?'

'No,' she said. She decided it was now or never. 'Have you?'

'Only one sister.' Giles's voice sounded amused. 'And you've met her, of course.'

'Have I?' Trina was innocence itself.

'Of course you have. Beth Garland's my sister. You must have realised that.'

'I thought she was your wife,' she said lightly.

He chuckled, but didn't elaborate. 'No, Beth's separated from her husband.'

They were out on the open road by now. Fields sped by, powdered with thin snow. Giles drove effortlessly, his hands steady on the wheel.

'Did you go straight into medicine from university or school?' asked Trina with interest a little later. He was older than the usual crop of housemen in their mid-twenties, and she'd wondered.

Giles shot her an amused glance. 'So you've noticed my comparatively advanced age, have you? No, actually I used to be an engineer. I used to design factories.'

'How fascinating. What made you decide to come into medicine?'

He shrugged. 'Lack of job satisfaction. I'd reached the top of the tree in my particular field—excuse the pun—and suddenly I realised I wanted to do more with my life than help to rot people's teeth. Sugar,' he explained. 'I worked in the sugar industry. I didn't begin to study medicine until I was nearly twenty-four.'

'Are you ambitious?'

'Extremely. I hope to become a consultant in record time. I have quite a few radical theories I'd like to put into practice one day.'

'Like Sam Barlow? Your theory about unconscious hearing?'

He nodded. 'Like Sam Barlow's case.'

'Do you think there's any hope he'll ever recover consciousness?' asked Trina. 'Now that we're out of his hearing, I suppose it's safe to ask you about his prognosis. What's your honest opinion?'

'To be perfectly frank, rather grim,' Giles told her. 'But there's still a great deal we don't understand about the way the brain controls consciousness after trauma. Hence my determination that everyone adopts a positive attitude towards Sam's recovery in his hearing. I take it that's still being kept up?'

She nodded. 'Very much so. The junior students have been thoroughly grilled in it ever since they started on the ward. It's something they'll always remember.'

He chuckled. 'Strange, isn't it, that one's first experiences and impressions have such lasting impact. I remember vividly the first operation I assisted for——' He smiled. 'An appendicectomy, of course—although I've forgotten most of them since. I expect you found that with your very first ward.'

Trina nodded, and found herself chatting easily to him about her first memories of working on the wards. He listened with interest, made perceptive comments, and asked her what she wanted to do in the future.

'I've no idea, really,' she said. 'I'm very happy where I am at the moment.'

'That's nice to hear.' He glanced at her. 'I'm glad to know someone's contented with their lot. There's so much griping about NHS conditions these days, it makes a change.'

'Now those I'm not particularly satisfied with,' Trina told him firmly. 'I simply meant I liked my work on the ward. NHS conditions are another thing altogether.'

'So there are changes you'd like to see?'

'There certainly are. More money spent on the Health Service, for one. And a much better ratio of nurses to patients.'

'Ah yes, I'd have to agree with you there,' Giles said. 'By the way, how's the nurse who went off sick?'

'Prue Gant? I've no idea. Her mother's been pretty ill, I think. That's no doubt why she couldn't concentrate on her job properly.'

'Don't you believe it.' He frowned. 'There's a more basic problem there, in my opinion. The girl's just not suitable material to take responsibility. Some people just aren't made the right way for it—impose it on them and they collapse under the strain. A couple of weeks off sick won't alter the girl's personality.'

'I think you're wrong,' Trina said. 'She'll be fine when

her mother's better and her finals are behind her, I'm willing to bet.'

'I hope you're right, for her sake. At any rate, a fortnight of rest won't do her any harm.' He grinned. 'I see you're still wearing your Joan of Arc armour!'

Halfway to Nottingham, Giles pulled the car into a little yard in front of a Tudor-style tea-shop and suggested a cup of coffee. Inside, they found a seat by the window.

It was warm in the tea-shop, and Trina found herself listening to Giles as he talked about his childhood while they sipped delicious hot coffee brewed with fresh beans. There was a cheerful log fire crackling in the grate on one wall and the atmosphere was cosy and relaxed. For the first time Trina began to feel at ease in his company.

'My mother died when Beth and I were quite young,' Giles was saying, his eyes on the flames from the fire. 'I suppose that's why we've always been fairly close.'

'Has Beth always wanted to sing?' she asked him.

He nodded. 'Right from her earliest years. She was always pretty good—what's called a natural.' He sighed. 'This wretched divorce business is being a nightmare for her, poor kid. I don't think she'd trust anyone else in a hurry.'

'Perhaps if the right person came along, she would,' Trina said carefully, thinking of Alan. 'Although I suppose that once you've been deeply hurt like that, it might take you a long time to recover your trust in human nature.'

Giles shrugged. 'Who knows? Personally speaking, it would take a rare woman to tempt me into marriage. I've seen too much of the unhappiness it can cause to go into it lightly.' He turned his grey gaze from the fire to look at Trina. 'That reminds me, I really ought to apologise to you for something, I suppose.'

She looked up quickly. 'Apologise? What for?'

He smiled to himself. 'For allowing you to assume I was married when we first met. Don't you remember our conversation on the way back from the shop when you flung at me that you don't go out with married men?'

Trina flushed. 'Oh, that.'

He looked at her over his coffee. 'I was so irritated at your high-handed reaction to me that I was uncharitable enough to let you go on believing I was married.'

'Yes, I know,' she told him. 'You thought I was a supercilious little thing, didn't you?'

'I did.' His grey eyes regarded her thoughtfully. 'The way you leapt to attack me the first time we met infuriated me, I'm afraid. And then, after we met in the shop and I attempted to ask you if you were doing anything that evening . . .'

'When I told you I didn't go out with married men?'

He nodded slowly. 'I was actually going to suggest that you might like to accompany Beth and me for a drink that evening, but you flashed at me so violently that I suppose I overreacted. It was a stupid situation and got everything off on the wrong foot. Shall we agree to forget it?'

His eyes held hers. Trina was conscious of a breathless ache in her chest, and her hands trembled on her coffee cup. Then she remembered the *poison* remark. 'By all means,' she said stiffly. 'I'm sorry I overreacted too.'

The ease she had felt in Giles's company seemed suddenly to have disappeared. There was an awkward silence.

'Perhaps we'd better get going again,' he said lightly. His mouth had gone rather grim. He signalled for the bill, paid it, and they left the shop.

Why am I always so prickly with him? Trina wondered miserably as they made their way back to the car. She was conscious of the fact that her own reserve had broken the spell of ease they had begun to feel in each other's company. Why was it? She had never felt like this in Alan's company.

As the BMW moved off again she kept her face turned so that she was looking out of the window. Whatever must he think of her now? Even more poisonous? She fought desperately with herself to relax and behave normally.

'What's your conference about?' she asked tightly, clenching her hands together fiercely in her lap.

Giles shrugged. 'Just a conference. The usual sort of thing.' His mouth was set in a hard line, and Trina didn't like to pursue that topic of conversation. The tension between them seemed to be building, and she wasn't sure why. She longed to say she was sorry for being so prickly, but one glance at his face set so darkly with obvious irritation daunted her courage.

He drove on for several miles, neither of them saying a word. It began to get dark outside the car, the winter daylight dropping swiftly into a gloomy dusk.

The atmosphere inside the car seemed electric. Trina felt a furious ache begin inside her. What on earth was the matter with her? He had tried his best to apologise, and she had deliberately made things impossible again. No wonder he thought her supercilious and poisonous! She was both—she admitted it freely, yet seemed quite powerless to do anything about it to put things right again.

The silence was worse than anything. It went on and on for miles, taking them further and further away from any possibility of easy conversation. Trina felt near to tears. She stared blindly out of the car window, watching the lights that rushed towards them through the darkness. The roads were busy as they sped through towns and villages and then out into countryside again. Heavy lorries went by on the opposite lane of traffic, their dark bulky forms thundering towards them and away again. Still there was silence in the car.

Unable to bear it any longer, she put out a hand to switch the car radio back on. Obviously the same thought had occurred to Giles at that moment—Trina's hand collided with his in mid-air. A spark of electricity seemed to fly between them as the car lurched sideways and, to Trina's horror, seemed about to go straight under the wheels of a huge furniture lorry coming towards them in the far lane.

Giles grabbed the wheel and wrenched it over to the left, narrowly missing the lorry. There was a loud blast of angry noise from the lorry as it careened on past them with its horn sounding like a furious burst of insult.

Giles steadied the car. No damage had been done, but almost immediately he turned into a layby and pulled to a violent stop. Then, turning towards Trina with fury, he stared at her.

'Just what the hell is the matter with you?' he demanded angrily. 'No matter what I say or do I can't seem to please you. Ever since we stopped for that coffee you've been sending out waves of something in my direction!' He paused, glaring at her. 'I've apologised to you for getting off on the wrong foot with you in the first place, I've done my level best to make up for it, and all I get is this stony silence. What the hell are you— a spoilt child? Some sort of brat that needs a good shaking? I can't make head or tail of you! And to cap it all, you nearly caused a fatal accident just now!'

Trina turned to face him. She was shaking. She stared up at him, torn by an impulse to jump out of the car and get away from the overpowering longing she felt to——

His grey eyes glared back at her, baffled and darkened with anger. She stared back at him, not knowing what to say or do. She was trembling all over.

The tension between them was unbearable. She groped for the handle of the car door. It fell open. Scrambling out, she ran blindly into the growing darkness of the layby, splattered with mud thrown up by passing traffic.

Giles jumped out of the car after her, slamming his door shut behind him. He caught her up and seized her by the shoulders, turning her to him furiously. 'Just what the hell do you think you're doing? First you refuse to speak to me—and then you nearly force us under a lorry!'

For a moment they stared at each other in the half-light, baffled, confused and angry. Then before Trina could answer him or say a word in her own defence, his grey eyes had suddenly darkened and his angry mouth had come down on hers with savage fury.

She opened her mouth to gasp. Her arms beat at his shoulders, vainly trying to fight him off. Then before she knew what was happening, his arms were round her in a powerful grip and she was melting in the ache and sweetness of a kiss that seemed to draw all the life out of

THAT HAUNTING MALADY 123

her, wrap it in fire, and leave her legs like jelly.

Giles raised his head momentarily, looking at her with grim satisfaction. Then he spoke, his words like a rasp in the cold air. 'Oh, I see,' he said bitterly, 'That's it, is it? I should have guessed.' And before she could say anything, his lips had come down again.

Trina felt as if she was drowning in honeyed flames. Never in her whole life before had she felt anything like this ache of longing, so utterly consuming, so glorious. She wanted to——

'Get back in the car!' Giles said grimly, suddenly releasing her, 'before I lose my control altogether.' He caught hold of her arm, pulled her roughly towards the BMW, and shoved her into the passenger seat. 'So that's your little game, is it? Leading me on so that you can accuse me of something further?'

He got into his side of the car and slammed the door. He was breathing heavily, staring ahead of him. 'This is not only dangerous,' he said icily, 'it's out of character too, for Joan of Arc.' He started the engine and drove off into the darkening road, his face beside her set like thunder.

Trina stared ahead of her, feeling utterly wretched. His kisses had reduced her to a quivering jelly, his wrath to a depth of misery so low that she felt she would never see daylight again. She was filled with shame when she remembered the sheer blinding joy she had felt when her mouth had opened under his. Did Giles think she had engineered this purposely and had led him on to get her own back?

He was driving angrily, dangerously fast. His mouth when she dared to glance at him was set in a bitter line. The car was approaching a town now, and he slowed down as they entered a thirty-mile limit.

Trina stared wretchedly out of her window, not daring to speak. This was unbearable, worse than anything that had gone before.

They were moving through street lights now, a row of shops, in a stream of slow-moving traffic. Gazing miserably out of the window, she suddenly saw the familiar sign of a railway station, and made up her mind suddenly. 'Please stop, Giles!' Her words sounded choked in her own ears. 'I must get out.'

He pulled in to a stop behind a row of parked cars. His face was set, expressionless.

Trina opened the car door. 'I'm sorry, I can't go on with you.' She grabbed her bag from the back seat, picked up her handbag, and got out of the car. 'There's a station—I'll go on the train. I—I'm sorry, Giles!'

Without looking back, she slammed the car door and ran towards the station forecourt and up the steps. Heedless of the startled shout from the ticket office as she ran blindly past, she made straight for the nearest platform. By some miracle there was a train waiting.

Doors were slamming, and the guard was in the act of blowing his whistle. Trina leapt on to the train, not caring where it went. It could take her to Birmingham, back to Norchester—anywhere to get away from Giles!

The train gave a jerk, then it was off, gathering momentum. She found an empty seat and fell into it, crying blindly, shaking with tears.

CHAPTER SEVEN

THE TRAIN rattled steadily onward into the darkness, its wheels pounding rhythmically over the rails. Lights flashed past outside the windows; stations came and went, too fast to see what they were.

Trina sank back into her seat, not daring to think about what had happened. It was enough just to get away from Giles, to recover her senses and to think. She had been insane to accept a lift from him! Insane. And yet if she couldn't ever know the rapture of his kiss again, she would die!

Whatever had gone so horribly wrong? She hardly dared think about it. She would *not* think about it! Think about anything, she told herself—think about Beth, or Alan, Mr Dalby, Sister Price, Mandy and Keith—anything but Giles and his kiss, the way his arms had felt as he held her, the way his lips had come down on hers—the way he'd stared at her, so angry and scorning! No, she must not think, she must *not* think!

She forced herself to practicalities. First of all, what train had she got on so heedlessly? For all she knew, it could be a non-stop express to John o'Groats or Land's End! The first thing to do was find out.

Trina peered round the seat she was sitting on. The carriage she was in was an open one and there were a few other passengers here and there, mostly businessmen with their noses buried in evening newspapers.

She opened her handbag, found her comb, and hastily

ran it through her hair. She found her pocket mirror and glanced into it—not too bad. Her face was blotchy and flushed, but a quick dab of foundation put that right. She put the comb and her compact back into her bag and straightened her coat, then went round the seat and approached the nearest businessman. 'Excuse me,' she said politely.

The man lowered his paper and looked at her enquiringly. He looked friendly, perhaps a family man with daughters of his own. 'Can I help you?'

'I wonder if you could tell me where this train is going,' said Trina. 'I—I jumped on to it in rather a hurry just now.'

The man gave her a grin. 'Yes, you did rather, didn't you? This is the four-fifteen to Nottingham—where did you want to get to?'

'Nottingham!' Trina exclaimed with relief. 'That's fine, I'm all right, then. Thanks very much.'

The businessman returned to his newspaper with a quizzical look, and she went back to her seat. Oh well, that was one problem solved—at least she wasn't on the way to Penzance! She could ring her father when the train got in to the station, he'd come and pick her up. Her parents were expecting her to arrive by car—she had rung them to tell them she was getting a lift, but her father wouldn't mind turning out on a cold evening for his only daughter. At the thought of her parents, Trina felt a warm glow which helped to subdue the ache inside her; it would be lovely to be with them again.

She was suddenly arrested by a further thought— what if Giles was waiting for her when she got to the station? He just might be, and angrier than ever at the ridiculous way she had behaved. Why, oh, why had she made such a fool of herself? Of course, she knew exactly why, she could face the truth now: because ever since she had got into the car she had been secretly longing —no, *aching* for Giles to kiss her, and *that* was what had made her behave so oddly. The shame of it flared in her cheeks and throbbed in her veins. And he'd been so angry! She would never be able to face him again.

What was so awful was that they hardly knew each other, and she had reacted like this towards him. Was this what love was like? A bolt of lightning hitting you out of the blue? Lightning? It was certainly some sort of electricity. When he'd taken her into his arms she felt she'd become alive, really alive, for the first time in her life, like a bulb lighting up! Was this falling in love? If so, it was glorious, all-consuming and utterly terrifying. However would she be able to face him on the ward again?

The train slackened its speed and drew into the station. People began to get out. The middle-aged businessman in the seat behind her poked his head over the top of the seat and gave her a wry smile. 'Nottingham,' he said. 'You're lucky this time. If I were you, I wouldn't go jumping on to trains in future unless you're sure where they're going. You might end up in Siberia next time!'

'I'll be careful,' Trina promised him with a rueful smile. She collected her bags and made her way out of the carriage and along the platform, being careful to keep her head down in case Giles was waiting for her. She just couldn't face him again this evening.

The passengers surged forward towards the platform exit where someone was collecting tickets. Trina suddenly caught sight of Giles's dark head above the crowd, and her heart sank. His angry eyes were scanning the platform. He looked livid.

Trembling, she dodged into a closed newspaper booth and hid behind a pillar advertising the latest political scandal. Train doors slammed, people filed past—a crowd of them at first, then thinning to a trickle.

Giles must have made straight for the station after her train had left! Trina imagined him driving through the dark, furious at the trick she had played on him, reaching the station, searching the crowd with those grey eyes that could suddenly turn so cold.

She waited for what seemed an age, getting colder and colder, not daring to emerge. Only when all the passengers had left the platform did she dare to peep again. This time there was no sign of Giles—where had he got to?

Trina dodged into a waiting room marked *Ladies* and made straight for the toilets. Through a small spot of clear glass in the centre of one of the windows she could just see the car park at the front of the station.

She climbed up on to the lavatory pan and peeped through the window. There was the BMW! Her heart began to thump uncomfortably.

She stood on the lavatory for a further five minutes, her eye to the window, aware of how ridiculous she must look if anyone had seen her. Luckily no one wanted to use the toilet!

After a long time she saw Giles stride angrily back towards his car, get into it and start the engine. She longed to call out to him, but bit back the words—she would rather die than face his scorn again.

She hid there trembling with cold until with her own eyes she saw the car lurch forward, turn smartly, and drive away with a roar. Only then did she dare to emerge.

The ticket collector stopped her at the barrier. 'Ticket, miss?' He peered kindly into her face. 'You all right, love?'

Trina nodded and fumbled in her bag for her purse. 'I haven't got a ticket, I'm afraid. I only just caught the train at the last station. I—I've been trying to avoid someone. Can I pay now?'

The ticket collector nodded and told her the fare. Trina paid him, her hands till trembling.

'Had a row with the boyfriend, have you?' the man grinned. 'Dark-haired man was looking for you just now. I told him I hadn't seen you, which I hadn't then.'

She looked up anxiously. 'Did he look very angry?'

The man winked. 'Bloody furious. Not the sort of bloke I'd want to cross in a hurry! Don't worry, he's gone now. But you won't half cop it when he catches you.'

Trina nodded miserably. 'Is there a phone box?'

'Over there, by the Left Luggage.'

She dialled her parents' number. It only took her father five minutes to arrive in his car.

Only later, as she sat in the warm sitting-room at home with her mother and father, was Trina able to think straight again. She sipped the brandy and hot milk her mother gave her and smiled wanly at them.

'All right now, dear?' her mother asked. 'You were chilled to the bone when your father picked you up at the station. Of course, you don't have to talk about it if you'd rather not. Just so long as you're all right.'

'I'm all right,' she assured them. Reason was returning with the security of home and the familiarity of her family. Giles would never be able to find her now; he had no idea of her address. She had simply told him her parents lived on the west side of the city, near the University campus.

'This doctor who gave you a lift,' her father said, eyeing her gravely. 'Oughtn't you to phone and let him know you're safe? Whatever happened, it was good of him to give you a lift.'

'It seems rude just to leave him guessing,' her mother added. 'Why don't you let Dad phone the University and get a message to him?'

Trina nodded. The brandy was beginning to have an effect—she felt a lot better now, and they were right, it was rude of her just to leave Giles guessing. 'Would you, Dad? He's at a medical conference that starts—this evening, I imagine. Just leave a message to say I'm all right and that I'll be going back on the train on Sunday.'

'He might suggest taking you back,' her father pointed out. 'I don't see how you can refuse without appearing downright rude, do you?'

'I can't face him,' she told them, anguished. 'I behaved so badly. If only you knew how badly!' It's ridiculous, she thought to herself, here I am, a staff nurse in charge of people's lives at work, and I behave like a neurotic child just because . . . He's right, I am poisonous, she thought miserably.

Her father went to telephone. Trina heard him dial the University number and ask to leave a message for a Dr Giles Bayne who was attending a medical conference that weekend.

There was a pause, then her father's puzzled voice repeating Giles's name. Another pause, then her father's voice thanking the voice at the other end of the line. He came back into the sitting-room looking puzzled.

'Is everything all right?' Trina's mother asked him. 'Did you get through?'

Mr Morgan frowned, looking mystified. 'There's no medical conference going on this weekend, whatever your Dr Bayne told you.'

'Are you sure?' Trina stared at him blankly.

'Absolutely sure. They checked twice. There's a hairdressers' conference *this* weekend and a chess seminar next Friday, but no medical conference, I'm afraid. Whatever this doctor of yours told you, he's come all this way for nothing, it appears.'

Trina closed her eyes. This was too much. Whatever did it mean? Had Giles come all this way for nothing, simply to give her a lift? It didn't make sense!

The telephone ran shrilly in the hall, startling them all.

'I'll go,' Trina's mother said, getting to her feet. 'It's probably this Dr Bayne of yours. I'll let him know you're all right, don't worry.'

She went out to the phone, coming back again almost immediately. 'Trina, it's Alan,' she said in surprise. 'Your friend Alan from Norchester. I think you'd better come and have a word with him. He sounds very worried, something about someone being admitted to hospital.'

Alarmed, Trina went out into the hall and picked up the receiver. 'Alan?'

'Trina, thank God I've got hold of you!' Alan's voice sounded tense. 'Is Giles there?'

'Giles? No, he isn't. What——?'

'Can you get in touch with him? You said he was at Nottingham University, didn't you?'

'That's where I thought he was,' said Trina. 'But why? Why do you want him?'

'It's Beth,' Alan's voice crackled down the phone. 'She collapsed on stage this afternoon and was admitted to the General about ten minutes ago.'

Trina stifled a gasp. '*Beth* was?'

'Trina, listen to me.' Alan's voice was urgent. 'She's in the operating theatre right now. It's imperative we get in touch with her brother immediately. Can you tell him to phone the hospital urgently?'

Giles! And she had no idea where he was!

'Trina, are you still there?'

'I'm here,' Trina said. 'But——'

'Will you phone him, or go round there? It's very urgent.'

'But I've no idea where he is!' she said, aghast. 'Absolutely no idea! He's——'

'But you said he was at the University, surely? Dr Rodney says all she knows is that he's in Nottingham.'

'Well, he isn't at the University,' Trina told him anxiously. 'We phoned just now. That is, my father did.' She thought quickly. 'Look, Alan, I'll do my absolute best to get in touch with him, I promise. He might well phone here in a minute.' But he doesn't know where I live! she added mentally to herself, horrified.

'But surely you know where he is?' Alan sounded irritated. 'Where was he going after he dropped you?'

'There's no time to explain now,' Trina told him, cursing herself for the hundredth time that she had been so stupid. 'Get off the line, in case he's trying to phone here. I'll get him to contact the hospital the moment I can reach him, I promise. Is Beth going to be all right?'

'I don't know,' Alan said grimly. 'Let's pray that she

is, that's all. Tell Giles to phone the moment he rings you. I must go, Trina.'

'Give my love to Beth!' Trina said urgently, but realised Alan had rung off before she could say it.

She put the receiver back on its hook and went back into the sitting room, her eyes wide with fear. What an idiot she'd been! If only——'

'Is Alan all right, dear?' her mother asked. 'He sounded dreadfully worried. What's wrong?'

'It's Giles's sister. She's been admitted to the hospital, she collapsed this afternoon.' Trina stared at them, anguished. 'Oh, I've been so stupid! Whatever am I going to do? I must get in touch with Giles. If only I hadn't behaved like a neurotic schoolgirl I'd know where he was now!'

Her father looked thoughtful. 'We could try the police. Do you know the registration number of his car?'

'I've no idea!' Trina forced herself to think calmly; blaming herself now wasn't going to help. 'It's a BMW, a dark red one. That's no help, is it? There must be hundreds of cars in Nottingham like that!'

'You could try phoning around the guesthouses,' her mother suggested. 'If he's not at the University, he'll be trying to book in somewhere for bed and breakfast. Unless of course he decides to drive back to Norchester tonight.'

The telephone rang again, making them all jump.

'I'll go!' Trina said at once. She snatched up the receiver, nearly dropping it again in her haste. 'Hello?'

There was the sound of rapid pips. A public call box—it must be Giles! 'Giles!' she gasped. 'Giles, is that you?'

'Trina?' Giles's voice sounded relieved. 'I've tried five

different Morgans in the phone book before this number! Where the hell did you get to at that station? I waited——'

'Giles,' Trina said urgently, 'please listen. It's very important.'

'I'm listening.'

'Never mind what happened this afternoon,' she told him, 'the important thing is that you listen carefully now.' Her voice wobbled on the last few words, and it was as much as she could do to remain coherent when she heard the icy note in his voice. 'Beth has been admitted to the General—she's in Theatre right now. Apparently she collapsed on stage this afternoon and was rushed into hospital.' She hesitated. 'Alan didn't know any details, but says it's imperative you phone as soon as you can.'

There was a startled pause.

'Did you get that, Giles?' Trina listened eagerly for his reply. 'I don't know what it is, perhaps her appendix or something, but Alan sounded dreadfully worried.

'Alan?' Giles sounded baffled. 'Who's Alan? Oh, your boyfriend. How does he know about this?'

'I've no idea. All I know is that Beth is in Theatre right now. Could it be her appendix?'

'She had her appendix out when she was twelve.' Giles sounded alarmed.

'They want you to get in touch immediately,' she repeated. 'Urgently. Will you do that?'

'Right,' said Giles briskly.

'Where are you?' Trina's voice was shaky. 'Do you want to come round here? I——'

'No, I won't, if you don't mind. I'll phone, then drive straight back to Norchester.'

'But you haven't had a meal or anything! Oh, Giles . . .'

'Never mind that, I'm tough.' There was a pause. 'How will you get back yourself? On the train?' His voice sounded grim.

Trina nodded, then realised he couldn't see her. 'Yes,' she said. 'Sunday. Oh, Giles, I'm so sorry, I——'

'We'll sort out apologies when I see you,' he said tightly. 'I'd better make that phone call. I'll say goodbye.'

'Goodbye, Giles,' Trina almost whispered. 'And——'

'And what?'

'And I'm dreadfully sorry. About—about today.'

'Ah well,' he said lightly, then the line went dead. He had hung up.

Trina went shakily back into the sitting room and sat down. Her legs were feeling dreadfully wobbly. She sipped the last of her nearly-cold milk and brandy with trembling hands.

'Well?' her father asked, eyeing her. 'I presume that was your Dr Bayne?'

Trina nodded. 'He's going to phone the hospital and then drive straight back to Norchester tonight.'

Her mother looked shocked. 'Tonight? Poor man!'

'Yes, tonight. And he hasn't had a meal or anything! I feel so awful about it, it's all my fault!'

'You weren't to blame, dear,' her mother said kindly.

'Oh, but I was!' Trina bit her lip. 'It was entirely my fault. I behaved so badly, like a spoilt child.'

Her father frowned. 'What I don't understand is this story about a medical conference which turns out to be non-existent. Whatever's the fellow playing at? He sounds a bit of a playboy to me.'

'Oh, he isn't!' she was desperately eager that they shouldn't get the wrong idea of Giles. 'He's wonderful! He's a first-rate doctor, an absolutely marvellous surgeon, and—and——'

'And you're in love with him,' her father observed with a smile.

'I can't be!' Trina protested, aghast. 'I've only known him a week!'

'What difference does that make?' Mrs Morgan's eyes were twinkling. 'I only knew Dad for a day before I came to realise I'd fallen in love with him!'

'How old is this Dr Bayne?' Trina's father asked. He winked at her mother.

'Oh, about twenty-eight or so. He could even be thirty. He didn't go into medicine straight away. He told me on the way up here that he was originally an engineer, but found that people meant more to him than machines, so he changed his mind and became a doctor instead. And he's a wonderful doctor too. He wants to specialise in general surgery,' Trina finished shyly.

'And you've fallen in love with him.'

'Have I?' Her hands were shaking. 'Well, if I am, he's certainly not in love with me. He's got every right if he never speaks to me again—you've no idea how badly I behaved.' She swallowed. 'He said he was married, you see—at least, I *assumed* he was, so I told him I didn't go out with married men, and that got us off on the wrong foot. I assumed he was married to Beth Garland. She's his sister, she's a wonderful singer . . . Alan's fallen for her pretty badly. Anyway, Giles asked me if I'd like a lift home to Nottingham this weekend because he was going—I mean *coming*, to a medical conference—at least I *assumed* he was coming to a medical conference, although actually, come to think of it, he said there was a *conference*, just a conference, he didn't definitely say a *medical* conference—so I said yes, but all the way here I was absolutely horrid and wouldn't talk to him, I nearly caused an accident—so I got out of the car and he was so angry he kissed me—twice! So then I rushed off towards the station and got in the train and . . .' She trailed off weakly.

Her parents exchanged amused glances.

'It's love all right,' her father said to her mother with a chuckle. 'A hopeless case of it, if you ask me. Nothing else could possibly be that complicated!'

'But you don't know how awful I was!' wailed Trina, anguished. 'And now he's got to drive all the way back to Norchester in the dark, and he hasn't had a meal or anything! He might get lost, or have an accident——'

'In the snow?' her father supplied.

She stared at them, horrified. 'Is it snowing? Oh, poor Giles!' She ran to the window and pulled back the curtain. Huge white flakes were falling out of a purple velvet sky.

'He'll be all right,' her father reassured her. 'If he's as capable a doctor as you say he is, a little thing like a bit of snow won't worry him. It sounds to me as if it's his sister who needs your concern, not Dr Bayne.'

Trina stared at them, wide-eyed. 'Beth! I must phone the hospital! I must find out how she is. Oh, please don't stop me!'

'In the morning,' her mother said firmly. 'You know as well as we do that she's in good hands, they'll do everything possible for her. Leave it to them—she's in the best place. Now, here's your supper. Sit down and be the patient for a change. And then you can tell us all about everything, this time starting from the very beginning!'

In spite of the brandy, Trina slept fitfully that night, her dreams reverberating with the memory of Giles's kisses. Each time his lips met hers again in her haunted sleep, she started and was instantly awake, only to remember that Beth was lying on the operating table in one of the operating theatres at the General, or in the recovery room that she knew so well, or in bed in a ward somewhere, being specialled, or——

She sat up for at least the fifth time. What was wrong with Beth? If only Alan had been able to give more details. It wasn't her appendix—Giles had said she'd had an appendicectomy at twelve. Adhesions? Not a perforated gastric ulcer, surely—Beth was far too young. Intususception? Surely not.

Trina looked at her watch in the darkness. The illuminated hands showed nearly one-thirty. Had Giles got back to Norchester yet? Was he lying somewhere in a ditch off the road, the BMW wrecked, snow falling and covering his unconscious body? Had Beth died on the operating table? Was Alan even now weeping silently and brokenly in some waiting area of the hospital, being comforted by Miss Earl? Was Giles—darling Giles, was his broken body being lifted into an ambulance, its blue light flashing rhythmically across the snowy wastes, the ambulance men shaking their heads gravely . . . ?

It was no good, she couldn't possibly sleep. Trina reached out and snapped on the bedside light. Who was on duty on Merton Ward tonight? Not Prue Gant—she was still off sick. One of the Bank staff nurses? Liz Burroughs?

Mandy! Mandy was working tonight, wasn't she!

Trina crept out of bed and tiptoed downstairs to the hall. Picking up the telephone, she carried it into the sitting-room and closed the door so she didn't disturb her parents.

She dialled the Norchester code, then the six-figure hospital number, and got through to the switchboard. Bill, the familiar night-switchboard operator's voice!

'Children's Ward, please!' Trina whispered urgently.

'Pardon?' Bill's voice sounded suspicious.

Trina spoke up slightly. 'Children's Ward, please. Bill, it's me—Staff Nurse Morgan.'

'Rightio, ducks,' Bill said cheerily. 'I'll put you through.'

The phone was answered almost immediately. 'Children's Ward, Staff Nurse Pearce speaking.' Mandy's voice!

'Mandy, it's me,' Trina hissed. 'Trina.'

'Trina?' Mandy sounded surprised. 'But I thought you were in Nottingham!'

'I am. I'm phoning from home—my parents'.'

'Why?' Mandy paused. 'Is everything all right?'

'Yes, it's fine here. At least—yes, it's fine. Look, Mandy, do you know anything about Beth Garland? Alan rang earlier, says she had an emergency op this evening. Is she OK? Do you know anything about it?'

'She went to Theatre late afternoon.' Mandy's voice crackled down the phone. 'She collapsed during the pantomime matinee—ruptured ectopic. They've put her in the staff sick bay—your side ward.'

'Ruptured ectopic?' Trina was staggered. 'You mean, she was *pregnant*?'

'She was,' Mandy told her. 'She's not any more.'

'But is she all right? Oh, Mandy, is she OK?'

'Yes, I think so. By the way, Giles Bayne was seen earlier on, going in to see her. Hey, Trina, what on earth is going on? I thought he was in Nottingham with you.'

'It's a long story,' Trina told her. 'Are you absolutely sure he was with Beth earlier?'

'Of course I'm sure—Liz Burroughs told me at meal break. She's on Merton tonight. Apparently Giles came dashing in at about nine, looking thunderous—perhaps he was just worried about Beth, but Liz said he looked pretty tight-lipped.' She paused, then hissed quickly, 'Hey, Trina, I'll have to go—Miss Earl's on the way to do a ward round. I'll see you.' She rang off.

Trina replaced the receiver carefully. Beth was going to be all right! She breathed a sight of relief. And Giles had got back safely to Norchester! That was all that mattered.

She crept back up the stairs and got into bed, pulling the bedclothes up round her shoulders. She could have danced on the ceiling for sheer joy. Giles was all right! That was all that mattered. It mattered even more to her than Beth's operation, Trina realised with shame. No matter how angry he was with her, no matter what storm of his fury she might have to face when she got back to the hospital on Sunday, Giles—darling Giles had got safely back through the snow, that was all she cared about. Nothing mattered so long as Giles was safe.

This time she fell asleep as soon as her head touched the pillow.

CHAPTER EIGHT

TRINA spent the following day trying hard not to let her eagerness to get back to Norchester show. Having come all this way to see her parents, it seemed a shame to spend the entire weekend with her thoughts elsewhere, and she tried hard to anchor them firmly to the present and brush all thoughts of Giles aside. But it was difficult; whatever she concentrated on, the memory of his lips was never far away.

Washing up with her mother after breakfast, Trina was constantly preoccupied. Gazing out of the window at the lawn covered with thin snow, she thought of Giles driving back last night. Shopping in Nottingham's busy city centre, she thought she saw Giles's dark head and broad shoulders several times, and found her heart beating unsteadily more than once. As she bought the lamb and other ingredients for the *rogan josh* that she wouldn't have time to shop for on Monday, she found herself gazing dreamily into the grey eyes of the butcher at the supermarket meat counter as he weighed up some fillet of lamb and wrapped it specially for her.

'Anything else, love?' the butcher looked amused. 'Cooking something special for the boyfriend, are you?'

'I'm—no, just a friend,' Trina said hastily, wishing with all her heart that it was Giles she was planning the *rogan josh* for and not merely Alan. She shook herself hastily. 'It's for an Indian dish. Not curry, something called *rogan josh*.'

'Never heard of it,' the butcher said cheerfully. 'I like Chinese myself. Can I interest you in a nice bit of mince?'

'No, thanks.' Trina put the lamb fillet into her carrier bag. 'Can you tell me where you'd have things like Giles?'

The butcher stared at her blankly. 'Eh? I didn't quite catch that.'

'I mean chives,' Trina said hastily, feeling her cheeks go a fiery red. 'Chives—and chillies. You know, spices and things like that. Cardamom. Cumin seeds.'

'Oh, I see, he's called Giles, is he?' The butcher looked highly amused. He pointed down one of the aisles to the right. 'You'll find spices and things down there. Chives on the vegetable shelves.'

Sitting on the bus on the way home to her parents' house, Trina nearly missed her stop while deep in thought about how she would face Giles again after Friday. Why had he said there was a conference at the University and implied that that was the reason for his trip to Nottingham? It didn't make sense. Could he have possibly made a simple mistake and miscalculated the weekends? It seemed hardly possible—Giles wasn't the type of person who made mistakes. He was far too efficient.

Thinking about it logically, the only conclusion Trina could possibly draw was that Giles had wanted the excuse to take her to Nottingham—and that clearly wasn't the case. You didn't purposely seek out the company of people you thought were poisonous.

Poison—the word caught at her like a thorn. Yes, her behaviour had been almost poisonous at times, she supposed—Friday evening had been a good case in point. However would she explain her behaviour away if Giles tackled her about it next time she saw him? How could she face him anyway, feeling the way she did about him now? Ever since his lips had come down on hers, his arms had gone round her, and the honeyed fire of his——

Trina jerked herself back to reality. The bus had drawn to a stop in her parents' road and was about to move off again. She jumped to her feet, only just remembering to pick up her carrier bag from the seat beside her as she dashed for the doors to get off. This is ridiculous! she told herself sternly as she thanked the driver and alighted—whatever am I going to be like on duty next Monday if I can't even concentrate properly when I'm a hundred miles away from him?

'There was a phone call for you, dear,' her mother said when she reached home, and Trina's heart did a sudden leap. 'No, I'm sorry, not your Dr Bayne—it was Alan. You don't have to ring him back. He left a message to say that—er—Beth, was it? Yes, that's right, Beth. That Beth is all right. Feeling groggy this morning, of course, but perfectly stable. He didn't want you to worry about her.'

'That was nice of him.' Dear old Alan, always so considerate. Not knowing that she had phoned Mandy in the night, he must have known she would be anxious for news.

'Are you sure he doesn't want me to phone him back?' Trina asked.

'No, he says he won't be there,' her mother told her. 'He asked me to give you the message, and to say he's looking forward to Monday evening. Apparently you're cooking him some sort of special meal. I think he said Indian.'

'I am. Something called *rogan josh*. The family in the flat below us is Indian—the mother gave me the recipe. I've just bought the stuff to cook. Fillet of lamb, the butcher cut it off specially for me.'

'You'd better put it in the fridge,' her mother advised. 'And don't forget to take it out again when you go home on Sunday! I suppose you'll want to go back on the early train?'

'Would you mind, Mum?' Trina asked anxiously. 'I—I can't seem to concentrate on anything here. I keep thinking of the hospital.'

'And Giles?' Her mother gave her a hug. 'Of course we don't mind. You must be anxious to get back and sort it all out.' She took the meat from Trina and put it into the fridge. 'Don't worry, I'll remind you about this just before you leave. Now, you just stop fretting about that doctor of yours and have a nice relaxing afternoon —there's a Deanna Durbin film on television. Put your feet up for once and enjoy yourself. You work pretty hard on duty, I know, and you won't reap any benefit of a couple of days off if you spend them agonising about things.'

Trina caught the first train she could back to Norchester on the Sunday morning, the lamb safely transferred to her carrier bag and packed in a polythene bag to stop it leaking. The snow had covered the fields in a sparkling carpet of white as the train sped through the winter countryside. She looked through the windows, thinking how beautiful the world was. Even the thought of Giles's probably icy reception couldn't depress her—just to see him again would be sheer joy. The little stabs of butterflies at the pit of her stomach alternated with surges of pure exhilaration at the thought of just seeing his face again. How could she have ever imagined she didn't like him? She adored him! She was utterly and hopelessly in love with him, she realised that now. Her biggest problem would be disguising the fact from him. Did it show when you were in love?

She got off the train at Norchester Station and walked the half mile back to the flat with alternately soaring and plunging spirits, knowing that the fresh air would help to put her thoughts in order. As she walked past the hospital, her heart began to thump. Somewhere in that huge tall building Giles was no doubt visiting Beth. What were they talking about? Would Giles tell his sister about her ghastly behaviour on the way to Nottingham? Surely not. It wasn't like him. No, he would simply keep quiet, his mouth would go into that grim line she now knew so well if she was mentioned . . .

At the memory of Giles's anger on the Friday evening, Trina's courage quailed. Now that she was back in Norchester again, he seemed more forbidding—the danger that he might well be extremely angry with her seemed more likely. What a poisonous creature he no doubt thought her now—now that he had had forty-eight hours to think about her calmly and objectively —wasting his time and his money on that ill-fated journey. Trina straightened her shoulders, bit her lip, then ran up the steps of the flat, determined to face whatever the next few hours had in store for her.

Mandy was asleep when she unlocked the front door of their flat at the top of the stairs, a DO NOT DISTURB notice on the handle of her bedroom door. There were no messages on the pad beside the telephone, and Trina wasn't sure whether to be glad or disappointed—she had half wondered whether Giles might have tried to contact her, then realised that of course he wouldn't expect her back until that evening. Perhaps he would phone tonight.

She had made herself a coffee and was cutting a sandwich for lunch when Sarah came in. 'Hello, love! You're back early. Have a good weekend with the old folks at home?' She helped herself to a coffee, then sat down at the table and watched Trina buttering bread. 'Make me one too, there's a dear. You look rather pale. Is everything all right? How did your trip to Nottingham with the delicious Dr Bayne go?'

Trina shrugged, reaching for more slices of bread. 'Bit of a disaster, to be perfectly honest.'

Sarah looked interested. 'Oh? What went wrong? Apart from Giles having to turn and rush back here as soon as you'd got there, I mean.' Without waiting for an answer, she went on eagerly, 'I expect you've heard the news about his sister. A surprise, wasn't it—a ruptured ectopic! Apparently no one realised Beth was pregnant, not even Giles! They rushed her in for a laparotomy, and when Mr Prosser opened her up it was obvious—her Fallopian tube was in a terrible mess, poor girl.'

'Poor Beth.' Trina passed over a sandwich. 'Is she going to be all right?'

'Yes, she'll be OK. But of course she lost the baby. I wonder how she felt about it—it can't be much fun to have your husband run off with another woman when you're in the early weeks of pregnancy. I wonder if he knew she was expecting.' Sarah peered at Trina as she took a bite of her sandwich. 'Are you all right, love? You're very quiet.'

'Yes, I'm all right,' Trina said wanly. 'Not a very restful weekend, that's all.' She hesitated. 'By the way, have you seen Giles since he got back? I—I was rather worried about him driving all the way back here as soon as he'd got to Nottingham. He hadn't had a meal or—or anything.'

'Yes, what exactly happened that night?' Sarah's eyes searched Trina's face. 'All we knew was that he arrived back here at the hospital at about eight-thirty absolutely spitting fire. Well, I suppose to be honest, more grim and tight-lipped than spitting fire, but he looked furious. Just as well he wasn't on call that evening—I'd have pitied anyone who got in his way.' She eyed Trina. 'You don't have to tell me if you don't want to, but did something happen between you two?'

'Something happen?'

'You know perfectly well what I mean. Did you have a row? According to Liz Burroughs, Giles was like a bear with a sore head when he went to see Beth that evening. And it didn't seem to be just anxiety that was bugging him.' She watched Trina carefully. 'What exactly went wrong between you? Come on, you can tell Aunty Sarah.'

Trina sighed and sat down. 'It was all my fault.'

'What happened?'

'Everything—and nothing. Giles said I was awful —rude and uncommunicative.'

Sarah stared at her. 'Rude? *You?* Trina, that doesn't make sense. You're incapable of being deliberately rude. As for uncommunicative—that's just not you at all.'

'Well, I was. I nearly caused an accident at one point. And then . . .'

'What?'

Trina couldn't bring herself to tell Sarah about Giles's kisses. 'And then I—I told him to stop the car so that I could get out. I made him drop me at a station, and I went the rest of the way on the train.'

Sarah looked at her, the sandwich poised halfway between the plate and her mouth. 'Trina, is there something you're not telling me?'

'Like what?'

'Like Giles trying something on, perhaps? Something like that? You're a lovely girl, you know, and he's a red-blooded man—and diabolically attractive too—I wouldn't be a bit surprised if he'd tried to kiss you. And you being you, you fought him off and screamed for your virtue before rushing off for a train.' She looked shrewdly at Trina. 'There's a distinctly guilty look in those inscrutable hazel eyes of yours, my pet. Aunty Sarah wasn't born yesterday, you know. Have I hit the nail on the head?

Trina nodded miserably. 'But it wasn't like that. The trouble was that I didn't *want* to fight him off! But he was so angry with me for leading him up the garden path that it all went horribly wrong. Oh, Sarah, what am I going to do?'

'You've fallen in love with him, haven't you?'

'Yes, I have. And it's hopeless—he can't stand me! He says I'm priggish—and supercilious—and he thinks I'm poisonous, you told me so yourself.'

'Oh, I don't think you ought to take that too seriously.' Sarah looked thoughtful. 'He didn't say it in a particularly nasty way. He said it more sort of—sort of pleasantly, as far as I can remember.'

'A *pleasant* sort of poison?' Trima laughed shortly. 'A poison's a poison, as far as I can see. No, there's no doubt about it, he can't stand the sight of me. And if there ever was the slightest chance for us before we went to Nottingham, I've pretty effectively ruined it after last Friday.' She smiled wanly. 'Thanks for listening to my troubles, Sarah. You're a good friend. I know I can trust you not to breathe a word of this to anyone, can't I? You wouldn't tell Giles, would you?'

'Oh, all right.' Sarah looked disappointed. 'I must admit, that had crossed my mind. But if you don't want me to, I won't.'

'Don't you dare!' Trina paled at the thought.

She spent the afternoon trying to read in her bedroom, but found it difficult to concentrate for wondering what Giles was doing. He was still officially off duty until tomorrow. Was he visiting Beth?

Trina abandoned her book with a sigh and turned the radio on very quietly, hoping to hear Beth's song again. It was one pop record she'd definitely go out and buy. Just as she'd grown tired of the everlasting beat of pseudo-American rock groups and given up hope, there it was—the now familiar throb of the single high note that introduced the song. *No cure for love, that haunting malady* . . . Beth's gentle voice came in softly on the third beat, *No treatment in the world could ever set me free . . . a hopeless case of that haunting malady.*

Trina listened intently, remembering the first time she had heard the song. No wonder Beth had sung with such feeling—abandoned by a husband who didn't want her and hadn't wanted their baby either. Well, Alan certainly wanted her; there was no doubt of that.

Alan rang at five-thirty. Trina picked up the receiver, half afraid it might be Giles and disappointed when it wasn't.

Alan's familiar voice greeted her warmly. 'So you're back. Did you have a good weekend off?'

'Yes, thanks.' She dismissed that. 'How's Beth? I haven't been able to think about anything else all weekend.' At least that wasn't too far removed from the truth.

'To be honest, I don't know,' said Alan. 'I thought you might know—hospital grapevine and all that. I'm hoping to go and see her tonight, although I realise they might not let me in. She might not want to see anyone other than her brother.'

'I'll find out how she is tomorrow,' Trina promised him. 'I'm on duty at eight in the morning. Don't forget you're coming to supper. *Rogan josh*.'

'What?' Alan sounded blank.

'*Rogan josh!* The recipe Mrs Patel in the flat downstairs gave me, remember?'

'Oh yes, of course. Lovely.' But his voice lacked enthusiasm.

'I'll be able to tell you how Beth is then, won't I,' Trina pointed out.

'Yes, you will.' He immediately sounded brighter. 'Do give her my—er—my regards when you see her in the morning, won't you?'

'Of course I will. Come round at about seven tomorrow evening. By the way, do you prefer white rice or brown?'

'Either's fine, thanks. 'Bye for now, Trina.'

Trina got the distinct feeling that his heart wasn't

really in accepting the invitation. She shrugged, hung up and went to have a bath.

By ten o'clock that night she was more than ready for her bed. There had been no phone call from Giles, and by nine-thirty she was beginning to feel unreasonably depressed. She told herself it was stupid to expect him to ring, but the fact that he hadn't done so made the prospect of seeing him on the ward tomorrow doubly worrying; he was obviously still angry with her. Trina felt weak at the thought, and wretchedly anxious.

She slept badly again that night, and was up at six the next morning, far earlier than she needed to be ready for duty at eight. She made herself a cup of strong coffee with her breakfast, hoping it would help her to think straight. It was stupid to be nervous, and not like her at all. After all, she might not even *see* Giles. Mr Prosser had a theatre list on Monday mornings that often went on well into the afternoon; Giles would probably be tied up with operations all day.

Trina took a deep breath, forcing herself to concentrate on the *Norchester Gazette* while she drank her coffee. I will not think about him, she told herself sternly. Trina Morgan, you're a grown woman and a staff nurse—this is ridiculous! She scanned the newspaper for news of Beth's admission to hospital. Had the press got hold of it yet?

Yes, here it was, a piece at the foot of the stop-press column:

> Beth Garland, currently starring in the pantomime Sleeping Beauty at the Royal Theatre, collapsed on stage and was admitted to the General Hospital on Friday. Miss Garland's role

as Princess Rosebud will be filled by understudy Clare Hamilton while the singer is unable to continue . . .

Not a word about the fact that Beth had been pregnant. There was a photograph of the understudy and a line or two about her career, but nothing further about Beth.

Trina arrived on the ward almost five minutes early. Liz Burroughs was still putting the finishing touches to her night report and there was no sign of the day staff yet, so Trina went along to the side ward used occasionally as a staff sick room and tapped on the door before entering. 'Hello there,' she said, peeping round.

Beth was sitting stiffly in the bed, nibbling at a piece of toast. Her face brightened slightly when she saw Trina.

'May I come in?' asked Trina. 'I'm a bit early for the ward. Oh, Beth, I'm so sorry about your baby. What a rotten bit of bad luck!'

Beth gave a wan shrug. 'Oh well, perhaps it's for the best, under the circumstances.' She looked even lovelier without make-up, her hair tumbling round her shoulders.

'Does it hurt very much where they sewed you up?' Trina asked sympathetically. The girl looked near to tears.

Beth shook her head, but a tear slid down the side of her nose. She dabbed it quickly away with a tissue.

'What is it?' Trina asked gently. 'Would you like something for the pain?'

'It's not that,' said Beth, her lip trembling. 'It's nothing, really. But I would love to have had children one day, and now I can't.'

'So that's what you're upset about!' Trina sat down beside her on a chair. 'What makes you think you can't?'

Beth bit her lip. 'Giles says they had to amputate the tube that the pregnancy was growing in, which means I can't have children, doesn't it?'

'Did Giles tell you that?'

'No, but——'

'Listen,' said Trina. 'You have two Fallopian tubes, one on each side. So long as the other tube is healthy, there's no reason on earth why you shouldn't be able to have a baby.'

'Really?' Beth's cheeks flooded with colour. 'Oh, that's wonderful! I—I mean, I know I'm going to be divorced, but you never know—in the future I might—I might——'

'Yes, you might,' Trina smiled. 'Have you got anyone in mind yet?'

'No, not at all,' Beth said hastily. 'But it's nice to know.' She looked up. 'Trina . . . I'm sorry, I mean Staff Nurse Morgan.'

'Trina.'

'Trina, will you tell me something?'

'Of course. What is it?'

'It's personal—rather difficult. I—I've been seeing someone you know lately . . .'

'Alan?'

'Yes, Alan. Oh, Trina, do you mind? It's been worrying me dreadfully. Giles says he's a good friend of yours—your boyfriend, in fact. There's something I must talk to you about . . .'

Trina looked at her watch. 'I think we both need to talk, don't you? It's eight o'clock—I must go for the Report. Look, I tell you what, I'll come in my coffee break, and we can talk. OK?'

Beth nodded vigorously. 'Would you?'

Trina went to report for duty. After Liz Burroughs had given her Night Report and gone off duty, Sister Price gave the ward Report. Mr Dalby was to discontinue his IVI this morning, to sit out of bed for longer periods and continue his physio exercises. There was no change in Sam Barlow's condition. Mr Neville had gone home, so had Mrs White. The other patients were making steady progress. There had been a couple of emergency admissions over the weekend: a girl with a head injury had fallen off her horse, suffered slight concussion and was in for observation—and of course, Beth.

Sister Price seemed rather thrilled to have a celebrity on her ward. 'We've put her in the side ward,' she told the nurses. 'She didn't want to be a private patient and we could hardly put her in a general cubicle, so the staff bay seemed the best solution. She would have gone to Gynae, but their side wards are both occupied with patients receiving radiotherapy.'

The nurses exchanged excited glances. To have a pop singer and actress in their care seemed quite an event!

'She's to be nursed more or less like a third-day post-op appendicectomy,' Sister Price went on. 'She can get up to toilet, and she's to be encouraged to move about after lunch. I think that's all. Staff Nurse Morgan, if you could do the dispensary . . . ?'

Trina nodded as they all dispersed to get on with the routine work. There were several day cases for Theatre and Trina found to her relief that she was so busy she hardly had time to worry about seeing Giles. In any case he would be tied up in Theatre at least until the afternoon.

The Introductory Block students were now on the wards for the whole day, and Trina was glad of their two extra pairs of hands. After the beds and washes were finished, she left Nurse Patel in charge of Sam Barlow's two-hourly turns and went to do the head injury observations. The girl's blood pressure was nice and stable, with no sign of the slowing pulse-rate that would indicate raised intra-cranial pressure. Trina filled in her observations on the chart, then went to do the ten a.m. medicine round.

She finished it just as the first day-case, a cystoscopy, returned from Theatre. Posting Nurse Stevens to keep an eye on him, Trina took Nurse Patel to the first coffee break. She sent the Indian girl on down to the dining room, then made her way towards Beth's side ward.

To her dismay there was a white-coated figure just coming out of Beth's room. Trina's heart gave a violent lurch. Was it Giles? Surely not!

To her great relief, it wasn't. It was only a Path Lab technician emerging with a request form and specimen bottle of blood. Trina dared to breathe again.

Beth's little room was fragrant with the scent of roses, and there was an enormous bouquet of them standing in one of the ward flower-vases on Beth's bedside locker.

'Aren't they beautiful!' Beth's eyes were shining. 'Read the card, Trina.' She was sitting out in a chair beside the bed, with a magazine on her knees.

Trina reached out for the card. *From Alan, with love*, it said. Trina looked mischievously at Beth. 'With *love*?'

Beth flushed. 'Lovely, aren't they?'

'They certainly are. Is that what you wanted to talk to me about?'

Beth nodded ruefully. 'I don't know how to face you, Trina. Whatever will you think of me?'

Trina drew up a chair and sat down. Beth was staring at her anxiously. 'Face me? Why? What's worrying you?'

Beth hesitated, then she said carefully, 'Trina, I don't know what to say. I've never met anyone like him before. I've only seen him a few times, but . . .'

'But what?' Trina disguised her amusement.

'I—I've never felt so—so *safe* with anyone before.'

'Alan?'

The girl nodded. 'He makes me feel absolutely wonderful. Loved and cherished and——' She paused. 'It's something I've never experienced before. I married Shaun when we were both quite young. You know we're separated, don't you? He left me when I told him about the baby—he said he didn't want children. Well, I've lost that baby now. But Alan makes me feel . . .'

'Cherished?'

Beth nodded eagerly. 'Oh, Trina, do you mind? He says you're only good friends, that you've never been anything more than friends, but——' she looked up at Trina, anguished, 'I feel I shouldn't allow myself to think about him that way, because of—because of you.'

'Me?' Trina smiled easily. 'Look, Beth, let's get one thing straight. Alan's right, he and I have never been more than friends. That's the absolute truth. We get on well together—we've been out lots of times, but——'

'But you're not in love with him?'

'No. I never have been. Alan isn't——' Trina checked herself quickly. She had been going to say she had never found him physically attractive, but perhaps that was a bit too frank. 'Alan isn't anything other than a very good friend,' she finished firmly.

'So you don't mind if——'

'If you fall in love with each other?' She was amused at Beth's sudden blush. 'Nothing would make me happier. Alan's a darling. He's calm, patient, and utterly dependable—he'll make someone a wonderful husband one day. But it won't be me.'

'Yes, he is a darling, isn't he?' Beth's eyes shone. 'Something pretty fantastic happened to us both, the first time we met. It was on the Children's Ward, funnily enough. It's something I've never experienced before.' She looked at Trina. 'What about you? Are you in love with anyone, Trina?'

'Me?' Trina felt her cheeks flaming furiously. Beth was Giles's sister, after all! 'No,' she said quickly. 'Absolutely not.'

'No one?' Beth's eyes were twinkling. 'Are you sure?'

To Trina's relief there was a knock on the door, then her heart gave a lurch—was it Giles?

Sister Price came in, bearing an enormous bouquet of more flowers; mixed ones this time: carnations, freesias and chrysanthemums. 'From your theatre people,' she told Beth, setting the huge polythene-wrapped bouquet on her knee. 'Aren't they magnificent?'

'How lovely,' said Beth, reading the card. Her eyes filled with tears. 'People are so kind.'

Sister Price eyed them both. 'Now then,' she said firmly, 'it's time you had a rest, my girl. And Staff Nurse must have her proper break from the ward or I shall have the Admin breathing down my neck!' She helped Beth back into bed, then shooed Trina out. 'Come on, off you go.'

'I'm going, Sister,' Trina grinned. She stood up, tucking her chair back under the bed. 'Cheerio, Beth. Don't forget what I said, will you, about Alan.'

'Alan?' Sister Price looked interested. 'Who's Alan?'

'Oh, a mutual friend of ours,' said Trina with a wink at Beth. 'The gentleman who sent Miss Garland those lovely roses.'

Sister Price bent to smell them. 'Mmm, wonderful! When I was your age I'd have fallen in love with any young man who sent me flowers like that.' She straightened. 'Speaking of young men, I've just had Dr Bayne on the phone. He sends his love, and says he'll be along to see you as soon as he's finished operating.' She turned to Trina. 'Why, Staff, you've gone quite pale! Are you feeling all right?'

'I'm fine,' Trina said quickly, aware that Beth was looking at her speculatively. Giles was coming to the ward! So there was to be no escape for her after all. She left the room hurriedly.

'Whatever's the matter with the girl?' she heard Sister Price say as she closed the door. 'I only have to mention your brother's name and she jumps like a frightened rabbit. I can't make it out.'

'Could be love,' she heard Beth answer with a low chuckle. 'But don't tell her I said so—she may not have realised it yet!'

CHAPTER NINE

BY FOUR P.M. all the theatre patients were back in bed. Leaving Nurse Patel to keep an eye on the last one back, Trina took Nurse Stevens into the side ward to turn Sam Barlow.

As they entered his room, Trina saw the tail of a white coat disappearing into Beth's room opposite, and her heart began to thump violently. Giles! If only he'd stay in there for an hour, she wouldn't have to face him before she went off duty.

She forced herself to concentrate on the job in hand. Sam was lying on his left side in the recovery position as usual, just as he had been left at two. They turned him over on to his right, arranging his limbs carefully and treating his pressure areas. There was no reaction; Sam slept on, quite inanimate.

'Poor man!' Christine Stevens looked at the prone form with compassion, but an answering frown from Trina cut her short.

'There you are, Mr Barlow,' Trina said brightly. 'Comfortable?' Her eyes met Christine Stevens' over the unconscious figure.

Christine tapped Sam on the shoulder. 'I expect Tracy will come and see you this evening. It would be nice if you were awake to say hello to her.' Tracy was his girlfriend, a thin girl of indeterminate age who came doggedly to visit him each night. There was still no response, and Trina sighed.

The door opened and Sister Price looked in. 'Everything all right in here?'

'Fine, Sister,' said Trina. 'We were just telling Mr Barlow that Tracy's coming to visit him tonight, weren't we, Sam?'

Sister Price glanced up at the clock. 'I'm just going for a cup of tea, Staff. Dr Bayne's in the side ward with his sister if you need him. I won't be long.'

Trina nodded. Nothing short of an earthquake would tempt her into disturbing Giles today! If only he would stay in there for another fifty minutes she'd be safely off duty when he emerged.

Before Sister Price could leave the room, the door opened again and to Trina's dismay Giles sauntered into the room. Trina looked away quickly, not daring to meet his gaze.

Giles looked towards the patient. 'Any problems in here, Sister?'

Sister Price looked round. 'No, I don't think so, Dr Bayne.'

Trina didn't dare look in his direction. She found herself trembling so much it was difficult to disguise the fact. Desperately fighting to maintain her composure, she stared fixedly at Sam Barlow in the bed. She felt rather than saw Giles's grey eyes flicker over her, his glance as electric as his touch had been.

'Staff Nurse?' Giles was addressing her directly.

'N—no,' she managed to stammer. 'Everyone's fine.'

'I've written Mrs Coker up for some Omnopon,' Giles told Sister Price. 'And the wedge resection could probably do with some too. He might as well have it four-hourly p.r.n. for the next twenty-four hours, he'll probably need it.' He looked at his watch. 'I'll be around for a bit longer before I'm off duty. Mr Prosser's got some relatives from Italy coming to dinner tonight, but the registrar's on call if you need anyone after that.'

'Right-oh, Dr Bayne.' Sister Price turned to go with him. 'Your sister's making good progress, I'm sure you'll be pleased to know.'

'Yes, I've just popped in.' Giles laughed. 'I could hardly see her for flowers!'

Trina was still trying desperately to avoid meeting his gaze. His very presence in the room made the air seem charged, the light unaccountably brighter. She wished fervently that he would go away so that she could concentrate on her job properly, yet felt she would die if he did. Still staring fixedly at Sam, she wondered if her eyes were deceiving her—he was actually raising an arm!

'Look!' she almost shouted, and three pairs of eyes turned to stare at her.

'His arm!' Trina gasped. 'Look—he moved his arm!' She bent over Sam. 'Sam! Can you hear me? Sam!'

Giles stepped forward and slapped Sam smartly on the cheek. His eyes were alight with excitement. 'Sam? Can you hear me, Sam?'

Sam gave a sudden hollow groan. He raised the arm again and swept it feebly in the air. Thrilled, Trina hardly dared breathe. Nurse Stevens stared with her mouth open.

Giles lifted Sam's left eyelid. There was an unmistakable twitch. He turned to them all, his face alive with excitement.

Sister Price turned to Trina. 'Neurological tray, Staff! Quick!'

Trina went to fetch it from the nurses' station, her

mind and pulse racing. When she got back to the side ward with it, Giles was still slapping Sam's cheek firmly and deliberately. As Trina put the tray beside his hand, Sam moved his head and groaned again.

Giles selected a pin and pressed the point of it gently into the back of Sam's hand. Sam gave an indignant growl. 'Come on, Sam!' urged Giles. 'Come on, old fellow—wake up!' He turned to Trina, his eyes alive with excitement. 'Say hello to him, will you?' He winked at her. 'A woman's voice might just do the trick.'

'Sam?' Trina's voice was urgent. 'Sam! Come on, you can do it! Open your eyes for us, Sam!'

To their enormous delight Sam blinked and suddenly opened one eye. It was unfocused, probably unseeing, but at least he had reacted. He shut it again and swore. The sound was music to their ears.

'Keep talking to him.' Giles spoke briskly. He put his hands on Sam's shoulders and turned the patient round slightly. Picking up the ophthalmoscope from the tray, he raised Sam's right eyelid and shone the light into the eye. There was an unmistakable pupil reaction to the light. He shone it into the left eye—no response. 'Never mind,' Giles said exultantly, 'at least we're halfway there! Come on, old chap,' he urged. 'Wake up!'

Suddenly, to their enormous surprise, Sam sat bolt upright in the bed. The neurological tray went flying, its contents scattered everywhere. Nurse Stevens dived to retrieve them as Sam stared at them vacantly out of his right eye. As they watched, the left one slowly opened too.

'Sam?' Giles's voice was charged with excitement. 'Sam, can you hear me?'

'What's going on?' The words were thick and slurred,

but who cared? 'What the bloody hell's happening?'

Trina found herself in Giles's arms, then hugging Sister Price and Nurse Stevens. They stared at each other in delight and amazement, and then speechlessly at Sam. As they watched, an expression of incredulity dawned on his face as his eyes focused on them.

'It's all right, old fellow.' Giles bent forward and patted his arm. 'You're in hospital. You've had a nasty crack on the head.'

Sam struggled with the bedclothes and started to get out of bed. 'No, you don't,' Giles said firmly. 'Not yet! He's bound to be a bit confused at first,' he said aside. 'Better give him some I.M. Sparine—50mg please, Staff Nurse, as quick as you can.'

Trina nodded swiftly and went to get it. When she returned with it drawn up and ready to give, Giles was struggling to hold Sam down in the bed with Christine Stevens' help, and Sister Price was holding on to his legs.

Giles took the syringe from Trina and gave it quickly into Sam's leg. Sam stared at them all aggressively. 'Bloody needles!' he shouted. 'What are you doin' to me?'

Nobody cared. They could have danced round the room with delight. Sam gradually quietened and lay back on his pillows, eyeing them all suspiciously.

Sister Price spoke quietly to Giles. 'Can you manage here for a moment, Dr Bayne? I need Staff Nurse to check some post-op with me.'

Giles nodded, his glance flickering over Trina. Now that the heat of the excitement was over, her shyness of him had returned and she dared not look at him.

She went back to the nurses' station with Sister Price, who was flushed with glee. Merton Ward had achieved something ITU hadn't done—it was quite a triumph for her! They checked the Omnopon together from the DDA cupboard.

'I think we'd better give Miss Bright some too.' Sister Price checked a second ampoule with Trina. 'Fill the book in, will you, dear, and I'll sign it later. I'd better get back to the side ward.'

Trina nodded, her eyes dancing. 'He was right, wasn't he!' she said, thrilled. 'Oh, Sister, isn't it wonderful!'

Pat Raynes peeped round the treatment room door while Trina was drawing up the first Omnopon. 'Whatever's going on in the side ward? What's all the excitement about?'

'It's Sam Barlow,' Trina told her. 'He's regained consciousness!'

Pat whistled. 'Wow, this I must see! All right if I go and peep?'

'Fine,' said Trina. 'Send Nurse Stevens back if they can spare her, will you? I've got to give a couple of post-ops.'

Pat nodded. 'I'll take Nurse Patel with me, if that's OK. She's been as involved as anyone as far as the positive thinking's concerned—she ought to be in on all the drama.'

'Yes, do.' Trina tried to snap the top off the second ampoule. It was tougher than she expected, and as she pressed on the glass top it suddenly slipped sideways and sliced into her thumb. 'Ouch!' She bit her lip crossly. She grabbed a couple of medical wipes from the box on the desk and wrapped a wad of them firmly round her thumb. It didn't seem to be bleeding too much.

Christine Stevens came into the treatment room, full of excitement. 'Oh, Staff, isn't it fantastic? He was right, wasn't he! Dr Bayne was right—it worked! Oh, isn't he *wonderful*?'

'Wonderful,' Trina agreed. 'You'd better come with me to watch me give these post-ops. I've cut my thumb and I'm a bit ham-fisted.'

Sister Price was signing the DDA book when Trina went into the office to fill in her name in the *given by* column. She looked up as Trina came in. 'He's quietened down a lot. I've left Nurse Patel with him to sit and keep an eye on him.' She looked at Trina. 'Are you all right, Staff? You look rather pale.'

Trina held up her thumb, swathed with tissues. 'I've cut my thumb, I'm afraid. Stupid of me.'

Sister Price unwrapped the soggy wodge. 'Hmm, it's quite nasty. You'd better pop down to Casualty and let them take a look at it. Might need suturing.'

Trina nodded, left the ward and made for the stairs. Blood was seeping through the wad of tissues and she was suddenly feeling rather dizzy.

She had reached the top of the stairs and was about to descend when she heard footsteps behind her. Concentrating on negotiating the steps in her bemused state, she gripped the banister rail.

'Trina?' The voice was unmistakable.

Trina found herself shaking uncontrollably. For some strange reason she couldn't seem to see properly, and she wondered if she were going to faint. The stairs yawned ahead of her, winding round into blackness. She staggered forward and clung on to the handrail.

'What the hell are you playing at now?' Behind her, Giles's voice was edged with irritation. 'Didn't you hear me call you? Or is this another one of your little games?'

Everything went black and patchy. Trina felt herself

reeling sideways. The wodge of blood-soaked tissue fell off her thumb on to the floor.

'What the blazes——?' Giles had reached her by now. She was conscious of his tall figure looming over her and heard the harshness in his voice change to sudden concern as he caught her in his arms.

Not fully aware of what she was doing, she clung to him, shaking. Even in her befuddled state she could feel the hardness of his muscular arms through his hospital white coat.

'Your thumb's bleeding.' Giles reached swiftly into a pocket. He wrapped a spotless white handkerchief firmly round the wound. 'How did you do it?'

'Ampoule,' Trina said faintly. 'Omnopon.'

'Do you feel dizzy?'

She nodded. Everything was swimming. She could hear a strange buzzing, bleeping sound. Was it inside her head?

'Did you get the Omnopon into the cut?' Giles was asking her.

'I don't know. I—I might have done.'

'Come on, darling,' he said, without further ado. 'Let's get you to Casualty.'

Before Trina had time to argue or object, he picked her up bodily and was carrying her down the stairs. At the bottom of the flight he deposited her on the steps and pushed her head down unceremoniously into her lap.

Trina felt his warm hand against her cheek, and could smell the scent of something comfortingly masculine —aftershave? Too dizzy to speak, she sat obediently on the steps, listening to the buzzing sound, wondering what it was.

Consciousness returned. Still shaking, Trina found herself ridiculously close to tears. She was aware that passers-by were staring at them with interest, and tried to get to her feet.

'You just sit tight for a moment.'

She obeyed him instinctively. Someone fetched a wheelchair from the corridor and she was bundled into it, her cap knocked off and tucked down behind her back. The dizziness came and went. She was aware of being wheeled along the passage to Casualty, then the startled face of one of the unit student nurses peering at her.

'Are you all right now?' Giles's voice spoke in her ear. 'I'll have to leave you—I'm being bleeped.'

Trina nodded, too dizzy to answer. She was aware of his warm hands holding hers and giving them a squeeze, then he was gone, his white-coated figure marching off towards the Casualty office.

By the time her hand had been looked at by Karen Bates, the staff nurse on duty, Giles had gone. Trina watched Karen as she applied a couple of butterfly sutures to the wound, wondering if she had been dreaming. Had Giles really called her *darling*? Reason told her he might have called anyone darling at such a moment—but he couldn't be angry with her, could he, not if he'd called her *darling*?

Karen finished binding up the wound, then applied a neat stump bandage and secured it with Micropore tape. 'You're lucky it didn't need stitching,' she said cheerfully. 'Nasty gash. Some of the Omnopon must have got into your bloodstream to make you go dizzy like that. All right now?'

Trina nodded. 'Yes, my head's quite cleared, thanks.'

'You'd better not use that hand for a day or two.' Karen was eyeing the bandage. 'When are you off duty today?'

'Five.' Trina looked up at the clock. It was already ten past.

'Are you sure you're all right?' Karen looked concerned. 'Stand up and see how you feel.'

Trina obeyed. She felt much better; the dizziness had virtually gone. 'Yes, I'm fine.'

'Would you like someone to walk home with you?' Karen still looked anxious.

She shook her head. 'Honestly, I'm perfectly all right.'

'OK.' Karen looked dubious. 'If you insist.'

Trina went back to the ward to collect her handbag. Before she left the ward she popped her head round the side-ward door. Beth was lying on her bed in a dressing-gown, eating an apple, her long red hair tumbled about her shoulders.

'I just popped in to say cheerio,' Trina told her. 'I'm off duty now.'

Beth waved the apple. 'Thanks for everything, Trina. See you tomorrow.'

'Sleep well,' Trina told her. 'And don't forget to dream about someone nice.'

Beth's face glowed. 'I won't, don't worry.'

Trina withdrew, without mentioning her cut thumb. As she made her way down the stairs towards the staff entrance, she suddenly remembered Alan. Drat! She'd better phone him and tell him what had happened —she'd never be able to cook a complicated Indian recipe with her hand all swathed in bandages.

* * *

The telephone was ringing as she climbed the stairs back to the flat. Good. With any luck that would be Alan; she could tell him about her cut thumb. He might suggest they went out for a meal instead.

She opened the door with difficulty to find Mandy on the phone in the hall. 'Oh, here she is!' Mandy said into the receiver, turning to greet Trina. Her eyes widened when she saw Trina's hand. 'It's for you. Giles Bayne.'

Trina took the receiver with trembling hands. It was difficult to hold on to it with the bandage, and she nearly dropped it. She transferred it to her left hand. 'Hello?'

'Trina?' Giles voice was cool, official, and Trina's heart sank. In spite of what she'd heard, he was obviously still angry with her. 'How's the thumb?'

His voice made her legs want to give way. She sank on to the stairs. 'All right now, thanks. They've put a couple of butterfly sutures on it.'

'But you're all right, are you?' He sounded anxious *and* angry, both at the same time.

'Yes, thanks, I'm fine. Thank you for coming to my rescue, Giles.'

Pause.

'You—er—you obviously got back from Nottingham without any difficulty, then.'

'Yes, I did.' Trina wondered if he was waiting for her to apologise about that. 'Giles,' she began unsteadily.

But his voice cut in over hers. 'Trina, we need to talk. It's hopeless when you're on duty, and the same for me. Could you meet me for a drink this evening? I'll be free about six.'

'Alan's coming round.' It sounded hopelessly like an excuse. 'I'm sorry, Giles, but I can't.'

His voice had gone suddenly cold. 'I see.'

'I've promised to cook him a meal,' Trina said lamely. 'Is it urgent?'

He ignored the question. 'Cook him a meal? With a lacerated thumb? I can't see you doing that this evening.'

'I suppose not.' She was about to say they'd have to change their plans because of her thumb, when Giles spoke again.

'Never mind, then. You're obviously tied up.'

'I'm afraid so. Is it urgent?'

'No, it's not urgent. Forget it. Goodbye, Trina.' He hung up.

Trina put the receiver back on its rest, misery tugging at her. Damn! Why was Alan coming tonight of all nights? That wasn't fair; she'd asked him round herself.

She lifted the receiver again and dialled Alan's number awkwardly with her left hand. Mandy had disappeared into the bathroom and could be heard humming to herself while she ran a bath. The bell at the end of the line went on and on—no reply. Alan had obviously left already. She'd have to explain about the promised meal when he arrived. What time had she said? He'd probably be along fairly soon.

She made herself a cup of tea with her left hand while she was waiting for him. Her thumb had begun to ache badly, and she took a couple of Paracetamol tablets while she sipped her tea.

Mandy came out of the bathroom, towelling her hair dry. 'What did Giles Bayne want? He sounded rather clipped.'

Trina shrugged. 'He wanted me to meet him for a drink. But I can't this evening—I'm expecting Alan any moment.'

'Oh yes, of course—your Indian thing.' Mandy glanced at the clock. 'Hey, is that the time? I'd better get a move on.'

'There's tea in the pot,' Trina told her.

'Great.' Mandy helped herself. 'By the way, what have you done to your hand?'

Trina explained. 'I've no idea how I'm going to cook the meal anyway, like this,' she finished, indicating her bandage.

'Does it hurt?'

'No, it's not too bad. But it's awkward. Heaven knows how I'm going to manage on duty tomorrow. I can hardly go off sick with just a cut thumb.'

There was a ring at the door.

'There you are,' said Mandy, sitting down at the table and helping herself to cornflakes. 'Perhaps Alan will take you out to dinner when he sees your problem. Might be your lucky day.'

Trina ran down to answer the door. She opened it on to the cold February air, half wondering whether it might be Giles on the doorstep. But perhaps that was too much to hope for.

To her surprise, it wasn't Alan who stood there, or Giles either. It was a thin girl, coatless and in uniform, carrying something bundled up in one of the hospital's familiar white cellular blankets in her arms. Prue Gant!

Trina wondered if she was seeing things. She peered at the girl. 'Prue?' she said doubtfully. 'Whatever are you doing here? I thought you were off sick!'

For a moment Prue didn't move. She stared blankly at Trina, as if taken aback for a moment, and clutched the blanket closer to her chest.

'Do you want to come in, Prue?' Trina was puzzled.

'What are you doing in uniform—and without a coat? It's absolutely freezing!'

Suddenly Prue lunged towards her and pushed past her into the hall. The light inside fell on her. Trina realised with alarm that the girl looked gaunt and oddly distraught, her eyes staring in her pale face. She was looking about her as if crazed. 'Where is he?' she asked in an odd, unnatural voice. 'It's no good hiding him. I know he's here. *She* said so.'

'Who are you looking for, Prue?' Trina's voice was a lot steadier than she felt. 'Who did you want to see?'

Prue didn't seem to have heard her. She jerked the blanket closer to her thin chest. 'She said he was here. I want to see him.'

Trina's heart began to thump uncomfortably. Whatever it was that had brought Prue Gant to their flat clad only in her uniform dress on a freezing February night, this clearly wasn't a social call. She forced her voice to stay level. 'What have you got in the blanket, Prue?' she asked gently.

Prue looked down at her bundle. 'Don't you touch it!' she hissed. 'It's mine!'

Trina was by now considerably alarmed. Whatever Prue had in the blanket, it was alive—she could see it squirming. 'Who do you want to see?' she asked gently. 'There's nobody here but Mandy and me.'

'You're lying!' Prue pushed roughly past her and ran up the stairs. 'I know he's here—his sister said so!'

Mandy's face appeared in the doorway at the top of the stairs. 'Is it him?' she called down breezily. 'That you, Alan?'

Trina forced calm into her voice. 'It's Prue Gant,' she called back to Mandy. 'Come on up in the warm,' she said kindly to the girl. 'Let me take the kitten.' It must be a kitten; only a kitten would squirm and give an odd little mew like that.

She put out her arms to take the bundle, but Prue was too quick for her. The girl twisted sideways, and the bundle slipped in her arms. As Prue gathered it up together again and ran up the stairs, Trina caught a quick glimpse of a tiny human foot!

For a moment she stared after Prue, too stunned to move. A baby! Where on earth had Prue got a baby from? There was only one place she could possibly have got it, and the realisation hit Trina so hard she nearly passed out on the spot.

CHAPTER TEN

'COME UP into the warm, Prue.' Mandy was speaking slowly and calmly from inside their front door at the top of the stairs. She came forward and put her arm round Prue's thin shoulders as the girl reached the top of the flight. 'Come and show me what you've got there.'

'It's a baby!' Trina managed to gasp. My God, she thought—she's stolen it from Maternity!

'It's mine,' Prue was saying in a high, strained voice. 'Don't you dare touch it, it's mine!'

'Come and show me.' Mandy was being incredibly calm. She led Prue gently into the sitting-room. 'Of course I won't touch it if you don't want me to.' *Phone Admin*, she mouthed silently to Trina over the girl's shoulder. She led Prue gently towards the sofa. 'Come and sit down and tell me all about it.'

'Where is he?' Prue looked about her with vacant eyes that blazed in her pale face. 'She said he was here! I can't see him.'

'I'll phone him for you, shall I?' Trina said quickly. 'I'll get him on the telephone, ask him to come as quick as he can.'

Prue nodded. She sat down on the sofa, still clutching the blanket to her. Mandy sat down beside her and nodded to Trina.

'I'll just give him a ring.' Trina closed the door on them. She stood for a moment, her heart pounding, then reached for the telephone and dialled rapidly. 'Miss

Earl, please,' she urged when the switchboard answered. 'It's Staff Nurse Morgan, and it's urgent.'

There was a pause. 'I'm sorry,' the voice said on the other end of the line, 'but Miss Earl's at supper. Would you like to leave a——'

'Then get me Dr Bayne,' Trina said without hesitation. Giles would know what to do. Darling Giles! How could she live without him?

'I'm afraid he's off duty. Dr Simms is on call if——'

'Never mind!' she almost shouted. 'You'll have to disturb Miss Earl's supper—this is an emergency!'

There was another pause. 'Who did you say this was? Where exactly are you phoning from?'

'It's Staff Nurse Morgan,' Trina repeated through gritted teeth. She gave her address. 'Will you please contact Miss Earl immediately and tell her——' She forced her voice to stay calm. 'Tell her I need immediate help at the address I've just given you. Then will you please telephone Maternity and tell them their missing patient is here.'

'What?' The switchboard operator sounded as if she couldn't believe her ears. 'Did you say—missing patient?'

'I did,' snapped Trina. 'Do it immediately, do you understand? This is Staff Nurse Morgan. MORGAN. Did you get that?'

The doorbell rang downstairs. Alan! Trina slammed down the phone and nearly fell headlong in her haste to get to the door. Alan had a car—he could go for help, for Miss Earl!

She wrenched the door open. Giles Bayne stood on the doorstep. He looked grim, his expression stern and forbidding. 'Trina,' he began, 'it's no good, I must——'

'Oh, darling, it's you!' Trina had no time to watch what she was saying. She grabbed at him and pulled him into the hall. 'Thank God you're here! She's stolen a baby—she's upstairs!'

He was instantly alert. 'A *baby*? Who——?'

'Yes, from Maternity,' Trina gasped. 'Prue Gant, the nurse who was sent off sick!'

He was up the stairs in three bounds, Trina close on his heels. 'Where is she?'

'In there!' She pointed to the closed door. 'Oh, Giles, watch out—she's crazy!'

He opened the door gently. Prue was still sitting on the sofa beside Mandy, clutching the bundle to her. A muffled wailing came from it. At least the baby's alive! Trina thought wildly.

At the sight of Giles, Prue blanched. She shrank back, cringing, her arms tightly round the bundle.

For a moment Giles just stood there, then he spoke quickly aside to Trina. 'What did you say her name was?'

'Prue. Prue Gant.'

He nodded; he was calm itself. He took a step towards the sofa. 'Hello, Prue. What have you got in the blanket?'

'Don't you come near me!' Prue's voice was high with hysteria. 'It's mine! You're not to touch it!'

'You're wearing your uniform,' Giles said gently. His tall figure towered over the sofa. 'Are you on duty tonight?'

Prue nodded, then shook her head. She stared at him out of haunted eyes.

'I hear you've got a baby.' Giles's hands were moving slowly towards the blanket. 'Where did you get it from, Prue?'

She flinched. 'My mother's dead. She said I could have it.'

'That's nice,' he said gently. Trina watched him, fascinated. He lowered himself to sit down on the sofa beside Prue, showing no sign of alarm. 'Is it a boy or a girl?'

She stared at him as if transfixed.

'What are you going to call him?' Giles asked her gently. 'It's a boy, is it?'

Prue looked blank. She turned her eyes from his face and looked down vacantly at the blanket.

'Let me have a look,' he said softly. His voice was incredibly gentle. 'It's all right, darling, I'm a doctor. I won't hurt him.' He made no attempt to take the bundle. 'Lay him down in your lap, so I can examine him. All babies have to be examined, you know.'

Obediently, Prue relaxed her arms, and the bundle dropped to her lap. Giles gently turned back the blanket.

Trina stifled a gasp. A new-born infant lay in the folds, its hospital arm-band round one tiny wrist. It was dressed in one of Maternity's familiar white baby-gowns. It lay there blinking dazedly.

'Put your arm round his head,' Giles said gently, taking Prue's hand and showing her how to do it. 'Let's have a look at the little fellow. My, he's lovely, isn't he?'

Released from its stranglehold, the baby began to cry. It waved its arms in the air and let out a wail.

'Got a good pair of lungs,' Giles said admiringly, still not attempting to take the baby from Prue. 'How's his Moro's reflex?' He turned his head to Trina. 'The Moro reflex is the grip all neo-nates are born with, did you know that, Staff Nurse? Look,' he said to Prue, taking her hands and putting her index fingers into each of the baby's fists, 'see how he grips your fingers? Lift your hands slightly—see how he holds on?'

Prue nodded dumbly, gazing at him with adoration.

Giles looked round at them all, as if addressing a group of interested students. 'The Moro reflex is always there in a healthy infant, even if pre-term. It's believed to be something we all inherit from our evolutionary ancestors. In the apes, of course, it plays a vital part in survival—the infant depends on it to hold on to its mother's fur.' He folded the blanket back round the baby. 'He's a lovely little chap, Prue. You must be very proud of him.'

Prue gave a shuddering sob that seemed to come from the depths of her being. She covered her face with her hands, her shoulders sagging brokenly with tears. Mandy bent forward and deftly removed the baby.

Giles took Prue into his arms. 'It's all right,' he said soothingly, 'it's all right, it's all right.' Prue clung to him, anguished.

Trina watched them, nearly in tears herself. His amazing grasp of what was needed to defuse the situation staggered her. She could only watch silently, awed by his compassion.

'It's not my baby,' Prue was sobbing. 'I took it from the nursery—f-from Maternity. I'm sorry, I'm sorry, I'm sorry! I didn't know what I was doing.'

'It's all right,' Giles soothed her. 'Everything's all right now. We'll give the baby back to his mother, shall we?'

Prue nodded brokenly.

'What was it that upset you?' His voice was gentle. 'Did you say your mother had died?'

She broke into fresh tears. 'Three days ago.' She bit her lip, anguished. 'The funeral was today. I—I just couldn't bear it. Everything went all funny. All I could think of was that I was going to lose my job as well, because of—because of——'

'Because of me?'

She nodded. 'I thought you'd make them sack me. You were so fierce that night, when I called you. And —and when—' she looked up at Trina, 'that night I gave Mr Dalby that cup of tea. Is he all right?' she asked brokenly.

'He's fine,' Trina assured her. 'He's absolutely fine. He's up and about now, and looking forward to going home.'

'Is he really?' Prue was shivering violently. 'So I didn't do any terrible damage?'

'No, you didn't.' Giles managed a wan grin. 'Mind you, I wouldn't recommend cups of tea routinely for two-day post-op gastrectomies—but you don't seem to have done him any permanent harm.' He stood up. 'Now, Prue, I think what you need is a nice drop of brandy and hot milk. I don't suppose you've got any here in the flat, have you?' he asked, turning to Trina.

Surprisingly, Mandy nodded. 'I have.' She smiled sheepishly. 'I bought a miniature yesterday for Keith —he collects them. I'll get it, shall I?' She handed the wailing infant to Trina, and got to her feet.

The sound of the doorbell echoed through the flat. Prue looked up, frightened.

'It's probably Miss Earl,' said Trina. 'Don't worry, Prue, she's only come for the baby.'

Prue looked terrified.

'It's all right, I'll explain everything.' Giles headed for the stairs. 'You just sit there while Staff Nurse makes your hot milk. I'll go and have a word with her.' They heard him open the door downstairs, then a low rapid conversation.

Prue raised adoring eyes to Trina. 'You're all so kind. And isn't Dr Bayne wonderful?'

Trina nodded. It was the most fervent nod she had ever made in her life.

There were footsteps on the stairs, and Miss Earl came into the room with Giles. She looked shocked, but Giles had obviously advised her to handle the situation with kid gloves. She bit back a gasp when she saw the baby in Trina's arms, then her gaze swung round to Prue.

'It's all right, Sister. Everything's under control.' Giles's voice was steady. 'The baby's perfectly all right; I've had a look at him.' He took the baby from Trina's arms and handed it to Miss Earl. 'I suggest you take this little chap and give him back to his mother. I'll explain everything in the morning.'

Mandy came in bearing a mug of hot milk that smelled fragrantly of brandy, and Prue took it gratefully. 'Good grief!' Mandy exclaimed suddenly, 'whatever's the time? I'm on duty tonight!'

Miss Earl consulted her watch. 'It's eight-thirty. There's a taxi waiting downstairs, you can come back with me.' She looked doubtfully from one of them to the other. 'But what about Nurse Gant? What do you——?'

'Oh, I think she'll be better off here for the night,' Giles said quickly. 'If that's all right with Staff Nurse Morgan?'

Trina nodded. It seemed sensible under the circumstances. They could hardly send Prue home alone.

'She can have my bed,' said Mandy at once. 'That is, if you don't mind, Prue.'

'How can you be so kind to me after what I've done?' Prue's eyes filled with tears. 'Oh, Miss Earl, I'm so sorry! It was my mother, you see. The funeral. And I——'

'That's all right, dear,' Miss Earl, said kindly. 'We'll sort it all out in the morning. Come on, Staff Nurse Pearce, we'd better not keep that taxi waiting any longer. Your ward will be wondering where you are!'

Mandy grabbed her handbag and coat. 'I'm ready.'

When they had gone, Miss Earl wrapping the blanket carefully over the baby's head together with an extra one supplied by Mandy, Trina found Prue a clean nightdress and showed her where Mandy's bed was. The brandy seemed to be taking rapid effect; Prue could hardly keep her eyes open. She fell into bed without even blinking, and was asleep almost immediately.

Trina put the light out and closed the door quietly. Sleep would do the girl more good than anything else tonight.

Going back into the sitting-room, she was shaken to find Giles still there. Somehow she'd assumed he'd gone shortly after the others. She realised she felt amazingly hungry; it was nearly nine o'clock and she still hadn't had any supper. She had forgotten all about her lacerated thumb too; the Paracetamol, together with Prue, had driven it right out of her mind.

Giles was standing by the window, his back to her. Trina looked at his tall figure, suddenly feeling decidedly vulnerable. She ached to fall into his arms, but that was hardly the appropriate action to take in the circumstances. Now that things had returned to normal again, he might well have stayed to demand a full explanation about Nottingham. Whatever was she going to tell him?

'You're still here,' she observed lightly.

He turned. 'Yes. Do you mind?'

Trina was too weary to be anything but truthful. 'I'm very glad you are. Would you like a coffee?'

'Very much.' He indicated Mandy's door. 'Poor kid. Is she all right?'

'Fast asleep.'

'Do you think you can cope in the morning? She's likely to be pretty tearful.'

'I'm sure I can. I'm not on duty until one. I'll see her home after breakfast, make quite sure she's OK.'

'I'm not on duty either.' His words seemed to hang in the air. 'I'll pop round in the morning and run her home. She really ought to see her GP. Perhaps we could sort that out with her.'

'Would you?'

'Of course.' There was a little pause. 'Trina?'

Trina hardly dared move. He was looking down at her with a strange expression in his grey eyes that made her legs feel decidedly weak. 'Yes?'

'Come here.'

She obeyed him, moving towards him as if in a dream. Giles put his hands on her shoulders, facing her squarely. 'It's time you and I had a chat.'

'Is it?' she said lightly. His hands seemed to burn through her clothes, and she felt her knees buckle.

'Go and make that coffee,' he said, suddenly taking his hands from her shoulders. 'And have you got anything to eat? I'm starving! I haven't had supper yet.'

'Nor have I.' They stared at each other as the telephone rang in the hall. 'I'd better answer it,' Trina said weakly.

Giles nodded. 'I'll make the coffee.'

THAT HAUNTING MALADY

It was Alan. He sounded elated. 'Trina? I'm terribly sorry about this evening. It went right out of my head.'

This evening?

'I completely forgot you'd asked me round for your curry thing—I've only just remembered. I can't apologise enough.'

'Don't worry, it doesn't matter a bit.' Trina disguised her relief. He obviously wasn't going to turn up after all. 'I expect you had other things on your mind.'

'I did,' Alan said warmly. 'I certainly did. I've got news for you. It may seem a bit premature, but Beth and I——'

'You've decided to get married,' she guessed.

'How on earth did you know?' He sounded amazed. 'Of course, we'll have to wait until her divorce is finalised, but Trina, how did——?'

'How did I guess?' she smiled. 'Not very difficult, really. Give Beth my love, won't you? Tell her I'm thrilled to bits for you both.'

'It won't mean the end of her career,' Alan was saying. 'There's nothing to stop her carrying on working for as long as she wants to, but——'

'Alan,' Trina cut him short, 'would you mind very much, but I'm in the middle of something. Give me a ring tomorrow.'

'OK.' He sounded surprised. 'By the way, is Giles with you? A crazy-looking nurse came into the side ward earlier, while I was with Beth. She was looking for him. Beth told her he might have come to see you.' He paused. 'I hope that was all right. She looked a bit odd, but she was in uniform, so Beth thought it was probably OK.'

'How did Beth know my address?' Trina was puzzled.

'I told her—I was there at the time. It was all right, was it?'

'It was fine,' Trina told him. 'Probably the best thing you could have done, as things turned out. 'Bye, Alan —I'll have to go.'

She went back into the sitting-room. There was no sign of Giles there, but a heavenly smell of spicy Indian food was coming from the kitchen.

She went to investigate. Giles was busy slicing lamb on the chopping board with the cake knife, and frying spices with onions. He had a pot of rice steaming merrily on the stove, and an apron round his waist.

Trina stared at him in amazement. He turned and grinned at her. 'Is this your recipe?' He indicated the folded paper on the kitchen side and held up a cup of mixed spices. 'This looks like *rogan josh* to me.'

'How did you know?' Trina's mouth watered. She felt ravenously hungry, and the spicy smell was irresistible.

'Oh, I'm a good cook,' he smiled. 'Had to be, in our motherless household.' He held up the knife. 'I'm not doing too well with this scalpel, however. And I'm having a job to find a retractor. I suppose you couldn't scrub up and assist?'

Trina could have burst with the feeling of joy that washed over her. It seemed absolutely right for them to be preparing a meal together. She found him a sharp kitchen knife and a spatula with which to stir the meat in the frying pan. You'd better watch your step, she told herself firmly. You may be in love with him, but don't let it show.

The *rogan josh* was delicious. They were so hungry they ate it off plates at the kitchen table—Trina just managing to balance her fork against her bandage—and laughing together at her clumsy attempts to eat. After they had finished the meal, they took coffee into the sitting-room and sat on the sofa together.

'Now,' said Giles, putting his coffee mug down on the floor, 'I think we need to talk business, don't you?'

'Business?'

He sobered. 'Why do you think I turned up here tonight? You and I need to talk, Trina.'

The way he said her name made her feel dizzy. 'Oh?' she said carefully. 'What about?'

'About a certain disastrous trip to Nottingham last Friday afternoon.' His grey eyes regarded her gravely. 'What exactly went wrong? Have you any idea?'

'Yes,' she said bravely, 'I know exactly what went wrong. But I'm not going to tell you.'

His mouth tightened. 'Why not?'

She shrugged, feeling her hands start to tremble.

'You've made it clear that you're not in love with Alan,' said Giles. 'Don't look so surprised—Beth told me. We do talk to each other, you know.'

'Do you?'

'So——' He looked at her. 'Could it be that you're in love with someone else?'

Trina felt her heart thumping wildly. She avoided his steady gaze. 'Of course, that's always possible, I suppose,' she said carefully.

'I wonder.' His voice was thoughtful. 'I wonder if——'

'What?' She hardly dared breathe.

'I wonder if an efficient and beautiful staff nurse —especially one that Mr Prosser held in high esteem, for example—I wonder if a staff nurse like that might ever find herself falling in love with a houseman?'

'Do you?'

'Do I what?'

'Do you wonder about things like that? I thought all you ever thought about was the patients.'

'Oh, I think about the nurses too,' he grinned. 'I wouldn't be a normal red-blooded man if I didn't, now would I? And nurses, of course, have been known to fall in love with doctors.'

'Have they?' Trina's voice wavered. She could feel a strange tide of longing pulling her steadily towards him, and resisted it breathlessly.

'Of course, with staff nurses it's different,' Giles went on. His breath was on her cheek, warm and masculine, and she dared not look at him. 'One expects them to be a little bit choosy. I don't suppose a staff nurse would ever allow herself to fall in love with a mere houseman, do you?' He paused. His mouth was inches from her own. 'Of course, if she did, it would explain certain oddities of behaviour if the said houseman gave her a lift to somewhere like—well, Nottingham, for example, in his car, wouldn't it?'

Trina was finding it difficult to breathe. 'It would rather depend on the houseman,' she said, hearing her voice tremble. 'If he was ruthless and rude, then I don't suppose she would. But if he was brilliant, ambitious, capable and—and amazingly compassionate as well, then . . .'

'Then what?'

'Then I suppose it's just possible she might fall in love with him.'

There was a little pause. Neither of them looked at the other. Giles picked up her hand and played idly with her fingers. His touch seemed to go right through her. 'How do you suppose I'd rate?' he asked huskily. 'The former category—that's ruthless and rude—or the latter?'

Trina swallowed. Her longing was difficult to control. Her hands ached with the electricity of his fingers and it was as much as she could do to hold herself upright on the sofa and not tumble sideways into his arms. 'Oh, the latter, I should think,' she said dizzily. 'Yes, definitely the latter.'

'So it wouldn't be impossible for a staff nurse to fall in love with me, you think?' Giles's voice had grown suddenly thick.

Trina shook her head. 'No. I should think that would be only too easy.'

There was no time to think—she was in the velvet hardness of his arms and his mouth had come down on hers. This time she felt no need to struggle—she abandoned herself utterly to the throbbing wings of his kiss.

After long blissful moments Giles held her away from him and looked deeply into her eyes. 'I've been in love with you from the moment you stared at me over the telephone in Merton Ward's office the first time we met,' he told her. 'Do you remember Mr Prosser's phone call to the ward? I asked you why you hadn't handed me over to him there and then, and you said there was no need until I'd seen the patient. That was the moment. Right then. I was lost.'

'Really?' Trina's eyes shone.

'Really. You drove me wild with your Joan of Arc act. You seemed so capable and efficient that you absolutely transfixed me. I had to fight tooth and nail to disguise how I felt about you in order to concentrate on my work.'

'So did I!' she said softly. 'But you were so forbidding and unapproachable! I too had to fight tooth and nail to maintain my dignity!'

'Your dignity?' He brushed her lips softly. 'Yes, very much a Joan of Arc quality. Now, what about that trip to Nottingham? I really must apologise for that. I let you think I was going to a medical conference at the University, didn't I? Did you ever find out that there wasn't one?'

Trina nodded. 'My father rang the University.'

'I knew my sins would find me out.' He traced the line of her cheek with a finger. 'I was so desperate to get some time with you alone that I made up the idea of the conference. You drove me wild with your silence on the journey, so that when you got out and ran, something just snapped. All my careful control went straight out of the window. Did I shock you dreadfully with my unbridled passion?'

For answer, Trina smiled. 'What shocked me,' she admitted ruefully, 'was my unseemly response to your passion! I thought you'd think I'd led you on in order to get my own back.'

'Your own back?' He seemed baffled. 'For what?'

'For thinking I was priggish. A supercilious little thing, I think you'd called me.'

'Well, you did seem like that at first,' Giles admitted. 'It was part of what drove me wild about you, your air of untouchableness. Anything else?'

'And—and for saying I was poisonous,' she admitted reluctantly. 'That hurt more than anything. I was a bit supercilious, I admit, but poisonous isn't quite so funny. Sarah told me she'd heard you tell Mr Prosser you thought I was poison.'

He frowned. 'I don't—wait a minute! Who's Sarah?'

'Our other flatmate. You know, the Theatre staff nurse.'

He looked puzzled. 'The skinny girl who's always gossiping? I know the one. But she told you *what*?'

'That you told Mr Prosser I was a poison,' Trina told him, her cheeks flaming. 'And that hurt. I was——'

'Oh, darling' said Giles, laughing easily, 'I warned you never to take any notice of hospital gossip, didn't I? Things get distorted so easily when they're second or third hand, you should know that. What Mr Prosser said, if I remember correctly, was that you were his *bella bambina* from Merton Ward. That is—a pretty child.' He paused. 'So I said that to me you were more *bella donna* than *bella bambina*.'

'Exactly.' Trina nodded miserably. 'Poison.'

'Not quite, my love.' He looked down at her, his face flushed with barely-controlled emotion. 'Your dotty friend Sarah reported it to you as poison, which of course it is. But literally translated into Italian, *bella donna* means beautiful lady. Mr Prosser knew exactly what I meant, of course, and readily agreed.'

His eyes darkened. 'Look, Trina, this is all irrelevant. I love you and I want to marry you. I don't want to mess about with any of this living together nonsense—I want you committed to me utterly and for life. My job here at the General may only be for six months or a year, and I want to know absolutely that wherever I go in this life, you'll be by my side. Say you'll marry me, and you'll make me the happiest man on earth.'

Trina nodded, her eyes shining like stars. 'Of course I will. I'd follow you to the end of the world. Just as long as——'

'As long as what?' he asked huskily.

'Just as long as you go on calling me darling,' she finished softly, as their lips met in an aching kiss.

Doctor Nurse Romances

Romance in modern medical life

Read more about the lives and loves of doctors and nurses in the fascinatingly different backgrounds of contemporary medicine. These are the three Doctor Nurse romances to look out for next month.

ON CALL IN THEATRE
Polly Beardsley

ISLAND OF HEALING
Barbara Perkins

ACCIDENTAL LOVE
Kathleen Farrell

Buy them from your usual paperback stockist, or write to: Mills & Boon Reader Service, P.O. Box 236, Thornton Rd, Croydon, Surrey CR9 3RU, England. Readers in Southern Africa — write to: Independent Book Services Pty, Postbag X 3010, Randburg, 2125, S. Africa.

Mills & Boon
the rose of romance

Mills & Boon

YOU'RE INVITED TO ACCEPT 4 DOCTOR NURSE ROMANCES AND A TOTE BAG FREE!

Doctor Nurse

Acceptance card

NO STAMP NEEDED Post to: Reader Service, FREEPOST, P.O. Box 236, Croydon, Surrey. CR9 9EL

Please note readers in Southern Africa write to:
Independant Book Services P.T.Y., Postbag X3010, Randburg 2125, S. Africa

YES! Please send me 4 free Doctor Nurse Romances and my free tote bag – and reserve a Reader Service Subscription for me. If I decide to subscribe I shall receive 6 new Doctor Nurse Romances every other month as soon as they come off the presses for £6.60 together with a FREE newsletter including information on top authors and special offers, exclusively for Reader Service subscribers. There are no postage and packing charges, and I understand I may cancel or suspend my subscription at any time. If I decide not to subscribe I shall write to you within 10 days. Even if I decide not to subscribe the 4 free novels and the tote bag are mine to keep forever. I am over 18 years of age EP23D

NAME _____

(CAPITALS PLEASE)

ADDRESS _____

_____

_____

_____ POSTCODE _____

The right is reserved to refuse application and change the terms of this offer. You may be mailed with other offers as a result of this application. Offer expires March 31st 1988 and is limited to one per household.
Offer applies in UK and Eire only. Overseas send for details.

The Perfect Gift.

With Love on Mothers Day

Four new exciting novels from Mills and Boon:
SOME SORT OF SPELL – by Frances Roding
– An enchantment that couldn't last or could it?
MISTRESS OF PILLATORO – by Emma Darcy
– The spectacular setting for an unexpected romance.
STRICTLY BUSINESS – by Leigh Michaels
– highlights the shifting relationship between friends.
A GENTLE AWAKENING – by Betty Neels
– demonstrates the truth of the old adage 'the way to a man's heart…'

Make Mother's Day special with this perfect gift.
Available February 1988. Price: £4.80

Mills & Boon

From: Boots, Martins, John Menzies, W H Smith, Woolworths and other paperback stockists.